CINDY SAILOR

AND THE HUNT FOR OWEN

D1248575

CINDY SAILOR

AND THE HUNT FOR OWEN

by
H. M.
SCHULDT

Professor Limn Books
Charlotte, North Carolina

To My Wonderful Family and Friends

CONTENTS

PRELUDE

The COVID pandemic began in 2019, and it changed a few things. Now it is thirty years later, and Cain is still an absolute supporter of social distancing and wearing masks worldwide in public. He is obsessed with having clean air and continually worries about unclean air. He often wears his oxygen helmet, invests in a new world currency, and uses personal drones for self-protection. His personal satellite is one among thousands. He carries his hologram cell phone everywhere and fears the frequent earthquakes. He takes nutrition seriously and wants to prevent cancer. He uses new infrared to avoid Dementia, and he uses many over the counter medical tests. For him, the quest for spiritual growth is self-centered.

Cain lives a private life and wants to control the world. He has been experimenting with illegal teleportation along with his buddy, Cricket. They have secretly tested on animals, and now they are ready to test it on a human. They promised Owen fame and fortune if Owen would participate as the first human to teleport. Cain's main concerns are unidentified flying objects and possible aliens. Owen has agreed to be the first human to teleport in exchange for a large sum of money.

Cindy Smith has been feeling anxious about getting out of the house. She enjoys cozying up at home and reading a good book. Ever since the pandemic hit thirty years ago, some people are still worried about unclean air. Her Aunt Judy wears an oxygen helmet when going out of the house to avoid getting contaminated. Cindy's a little stressed out about where to go to college and what to do with her life. She likes to figure things out, but she does not like to cause a scene in public. Other than reading books, she goes to the movies with her older brother and his friends from time to time.

Her parents are private and keep to themselves. This seclusion and loneliness of theirs concerns her a great deal. Her mother does yardwork by herself, and her father owns a motorcycle business where he takes the family dog to work each day. When she gets older, Cindy does not want to be like her older brother, her parents, or Aunt Judy, so for now, she stays busy with reading and doing logic puzzles. She is worried about getting fat, and she doesn't like it when anyone tells her to get her hair out of her face. She wonders about the meaning of life and ponders what might happen after a person dies. She continually fights off having panic attacks.

1

POPCORN BATTLE

Cindy's World Saturday, March 14, 2054

I tune out the ring of my brother's phone as I look at mine. A national news report says, "Falling Stars Seen Last Night in Ten Locations."

Oh, I saw one! It was amazing! I gaze at a photo. I tap on it and a hologram jumps up. It looks more spectacular than the photo.

"Cindy!" The tone in my brother's voice sounds much more urgent than his normal dry humor.

I head to the family room. He is sitting on the couch with his superphone XXXII.

I hope he isn't pulling another one of his pranks.

"Something happened." His eyes open wide like an owl. His furrowed eyebrows tell me he has disturbing news.

"What? What is it?"

"I'll call you back." He tells someone and hangs up.

I wait as he hesitates.

"Ok, take a deep breath," he said in a matter-of-fact tone. "A meteor strike hit Asia. Check your phone. They're saying these huge meteorites came down like bombs. Huge rocks. Mega rocks, they call 'em."

His calm demeanor somehow helps me to remain calm. "Oh. Is everyone ok?"

"No," he says. "The body count is already over a thousand."

I pause. "Oh, no. Are they going to land over here?"

"The bodies?"

"No! The rocks! How can you joke around at a time like this?"

"It says here that we might get some falling stars tonight, but they don't really know."

"I'm staying in today." I sit in our father's club chair.

2

"You know, I'm not going to be cooped up in the house. Aunt Judy has agoraphobia, and she stays home all the time. The White House is saying, 'Go about your business'."

"Should we still go see the movie?" I ask, hesitating any trip outside.

"I'm not going to miss it. It's sold out. Seats are first come, first serve. Let's go early and wait in line." His sleek wavy hair flares up on top and fades low on the sides.

"Ok." *I have all day to read then and stay inside.*

I head to the kitchen.

Oh, good! We have enough for today anyway. I reach into our refrigerator, grab a sweet tea, and take the last blueberry yogurt. I check the calories. I see no one has moved the digital clock forward yet. Gee. It's been a whole week.

"Hey! How do you change the clock on the microwave?" I yell to my older brother in the other room. I take another bite of yogurt. My low ponytail is the best way to keep all my golden blond hair out of my face. I'm not going to have another boy tell me to push my hair off my face.

My mother rushes by and heads for the front door. She yells, "Cindy, it's nice outside! Get out and go do something!"

"Like what?" I yell back.

"Take the dog for a walk!"

"No! I don't want to."

"Come help me plant flowers!" She says.

"No. I don't want to!" I say.

My parents live day by day in considerable seclusion. We don't even know our neighbors. Mom and dad value a spirit of kindness and indulgence during their busy stage of life, but they keep to themselves. It makes me discern how fortunate I am compared to other families with dry yards and empty cupboards.

"I'm planting the marigolds before they die!" Mom says and walks outside.

Maybe I can change it. Glancing at the digital numbers on the microwave clock, I consider letting someone else change it. No. I want to start doing adult things. *It can't be that difficult, right?* I might as well be the first one in this family to do it. With no one around, at least no one will laugh at me if I can't figure it out.

"Hey, how do you change the clock on the microwave?" I yell again.

No answer from my brother so I press 7:32 and then AM. Then I press the clock button. *That's it. See? Being an adult isn't that difficult. Wait. Why did the time change back? Whatever.*

It sounds quiet this morning except for a Carolina Chickadee who sings a four-note whistle in our backyard. I like how the morning sun looks beautiful out the window. I take another bite of yogurt. Cherry blossom season is my favorite time of year.

I really don't like moving into the triple digits. I need to eat less. Just a few more bites.

I see my brother's video camera after yesterday's shooting. His homemade Alfred Hitchcock style movie, Raven, is supposed to be scary. I think he better keep working on it in movie college. The action of strange behavior is his main theme and interest. His dream of all dreams is to become a great movie producer.

I'll give it one more try. Maybe press the clock button and then the start button.

There! It worked!

I read another page, sitting at the kitchen table. I turn the page and glance out the window again.

What am I going to do today? It's Saturday. Oh, yeah, I have math homework. It'll have to wait. I told my brother I'd go to the cinema with him and his friends. I really want to see that new movie tonight, Prison Island.

Cinema Six

Piper and I arrive early and find a place to park his Jeep. The air feels nice and crisp in the twilight hour. I see the line extend from the front door. My half-up top-knot hairstyle is keeping the hair off my face.

I think we are early enough, and we'll get some good seats.

While standing in line, I overhear several people talking about what happened this morning. It's strange that no one seems concerned if mega rocks will land in our city. After a while, Piper's two friends join us in line. I meet Vinny Brusco's girlfriend, Stella, for the first time.

"Did you hear about what happened in Asia?" I ask.

"That's too bad." Vinny's dark hair is smooth and slicked back. His small-trimmed beard makes his oval face look pointy on his chin. He grins. His lavender button up is untucked. "We got it good. Ain't seen no rocks flyin' 'round here."

Vinny and Piper laugh in unison. Vinny is wearing those shiny black leather shoes again. I notice he often looks down at them.

6

Piper and Vinny do not seem concerned in the least bit. They clearly want to have a good time. I quickly learn Stella is completely set on having a good time. I want to have a good time, too, but I'm still feeling worried like something bad is going to happen. I don't want to talk about it because Piper will make fun of me again.

"This is going to be fun!" Stella says, kissing Vinny on the cheek next to his thin, pointy ended mustache. "What's *Prison Island* about?"

Vinny grins again. I can tell he loves her attention. "Uh, a prison that's on an island."

Vinny and Piper laugh again. Stella seems to like anything Vinny says.

I've been waiting a long time to see this movie. "It's about an inmate who thinks he's a doctor sent to an island to help other inmates."

The line grows and snakes around the building. Someone behind us is wearing a new Smart Helmet XV and getting a lot of attention. He flips the eye shield up and begins explaining the benefits of it. "It keeps viruses out, and the infrared light prevents Dementia and Alzheimer's."

Piper leans in. "That's what Aunt Judy is getting."

I look at the helmet and wonder how much clean oxygen he is getting. I take a deep breath of fresh air.

"We're next." Piper shows the ticket on his phone to the person at the door. We each follow, phone in hand.

"Thank you, Vinny. I want to get some popcorn," Stella says in a flirty tone.

"My wallet is dead 'till tomorrow," Vinny says.

"Fine. I'll pay," Stella says in a regular tone. Her dark beach-wave hair strolls over her shoulders.

Stella and I stand in a short line at the concession-stand.

"I'm having a kitchen party, want to come?" Stella says to me as she approaches the counter.

"Uh, send me the details," I say.

"Next, please!" says the worker behind the counter.

"I'll have a popcorn and a coke," Stella says.

The worker returns with the items and rings her up. "That'll be 27 tokens."

"What?!" Stella gasps.

"The Bucket costs more, but you get to keep the Bucket, and the refills are only 5 tokens."

"I don't want a refill." Stella shows her phone and quickly pays with her digital currency. She looks at me, rich brown eyes darting.

The cashier points a scanner at her electronic wallet until he hears a quiet beep. "Thank you. Next, please!"

"Wait! The menu board says you should ha' charged me 18 tokens."

"No, that's for the special." The cashier looks past Stella.

"You should'a rung me up for the popcorn special! And you were supposed to give me some candy, too, for the special." Stella's voice grew louder than normal.

"I'm sorry. I have to help the next customer. Next, please!"

"You should'a given me the *popcorn special!* What, are you ripping me off now? I WANNA SEE THE MANAGER! I'm not leaving until you go get your manager. At least give me the M&Ms or the Sno Caps!"

"I'll be right back." Immediately, the worker walks away.

Stella turns to me and I look down, feeling embarrassed.

I look around and see a lady huff, roll her eyes, and look away. I see Piper and Vinny waiting in the distance, laughing about something. I can only imagine about what. Stella leans into me. "That guy ripped me off, and I'm not letting him get away with it. Here, hold this."

I shrug and take the Bucket. I don't want to add anything else to this dramatic situation.

I see the manager shuffling quickly behind the worker. He motions for us to meet him on our side of the counter.

"Hello," says the manager. "Please step over here."

We follow.

He continues. "What seems to be the issue?"

"This guy ripped me off and I should'a only paid 18 tokens for the popcorn special. Plus, he should'a given me M&Ms."

"I'm so sorry that happened. You're right. It looks like you got the popcorn and a coke. All sales are final. We have no refunds. Here are two free tickets and some M&Ms for you. Please accept our apology."

Stella looks unsatisfied. "But you ruined my night, and I'm with three of my friends. We need four tickets to make it even."

The manager hands two more tickets to Stella. She takes them and we begin to walk away.

"But she didn't ask for the *special*. The special doesn't include the Bucket," the cashier says to the manager.

I hear the cashier speak to the manager as we are walking away.

Stella turns, snaps her fingers, and points at them. "The customer's always right! You oughta' know betta'!"

We walk away with free tickets. Stella grins as her coppery-gold eye shadow sparkles. She makes me carry the Bucket. I see Stella's act of disapproval has quickly come to an end. She flashes the free tickets at me, lifts her perfectly groomed eyebrows, and looks at her new prize.

I don't want to get on her bad side.

During the movie, I feel a rumble.

I lean into Pipe. "Did you feel that?"

"What?" he asks.

"My chair rumbled."

"It's the loudspeaker." He places his pointer finger up to his lips and mouths something. "Shh."

The audience is packed in with not a chair to spare. No one seems to be concerned about a rumble that felt like an earthquake.

"Wow! I loved that movie!" I say. It made me forget all about the rumbling I felt in my seat.

"What a surprise ending!" Piper says.

"I didn't see it comin'." Vinny says.

"That was a great movie! And we have free tickets to come back!" Stella says proudly.

We walk outside.

I hear a little boy call out. "Look, mommy!"

"Oh," she responds, "it's a falling star!"

I point up at the sky. "You guys! Look!"

"Well, look at that. You don't see that very often," Vinny says.

We watch a falling star disappear into the night sky. It reminds me of what happened earlier today.

Piper and Vinny check their phones.

"Hey. It says a strike hit our city," Piper says in a sober tone. "We had an earthquake at 8:15."

I hear a firetruck siren off in the distance.

We say good-bye and head home.

Dear Diary,

I met Stella. She managed to get four free tickets to see another movie. Something bad happened. Mega rocks hit Earth. It hit parts of North America while we were watching *Prison Island.* I felt a rumble in my seat. It was another earthquake. Magnitude 5. Michigan got a rock hit. Remember to check the earthquake news and the mega rock news. Reports say we will keep getting hit this month. Why can't someone do something about it?!

Friday, April 17, 2054

My phone buzzes. It's my brother. I tap on the answer button.

"Hey, have you seen the preview for *Unexpected Suspect*?"

"Yeah, it looks really good!" I say.

"What's it about? The camera angles are supposed to be really good."

"It's a thriller about a girl, Norma, who goes out on a blind date with a new friend and two strange boys. One of the boys is murdered, and Norma is accused of the crime. It's getting good reviews. At the very end, Norma discovers the unlikely suspect..."

He cuts me off. "Now don't spoil the ending."

"I'm not! Stop punishing me. I'm just telling you what it's about. You asked!"

"I'm not punishing you. Stella has free tickets from last time. They invited us. Want to go? You really need to get out of the house. I want to see all the camera angles."

I really want to see this movie, but I didn't feel comfortable with Stella last time. It's been a whole month since her humiliating episode. I doubt she has changed any.

Maybe I'll go see it with Aunt Judy. She's nice and quiet. She keeps to herself most of the time. "When are they going?"

"Tomorrow."

Not sure if I should go. My book is getting really good, but I want to see that movie. It's been boring around here, so maybe I'll go. I want to see the movie, but I don't want to be around Stella. She's nice and all, but I don't want to be around if she lashes out again. Well, maybe I need a break from my book. "Ok. I'll go."

Dear Diary,

I'm going to see *Unexpected Suspect* tomorrow with my brother, Vinny, and Stella. Sounds like a good movie. I hope Stella doesn't ask for popcorn again. Do not go to the concession stand! They all have a good time together. I should just go. The strikes caused a lot of damage last month. News report says satellites went out in the Middle East. No more satellite wars! Stop worrying! Stop stressing out! Life goes on, right? Does life even care how I feel? Still don't know what I'm going to study in college. Find out how to stop stressing.

Stella hands four free tickets to the guy at the door. I am feeling unsettled again like something bad is going to happen. I exhale a sigh of relief when I find out no one wants to get popcorn. The movie begins and our eyes are locked onto the big screen. My half-up double space-buns are keeping the hair off my face. Half-way through the movie, I feel a rumble. It lasts for only a few seconds. I lean into Pipe. "Was that an earthquake?"

He shrugs. "It stopped."

We watch the movie with our eyes glued all the way to the end.

I'm the first to stand up in the dark.

"What a great movie!" Stella expresses how much she liked certain parts as we walk outside.

I agree with her. "Norma reminded me of a cat."

"Her black eyeliner! I loved it!" Stella says.

"That was a chick flick." Vinny speaks with a joyful tone and smiles.

"Hey, did you guys feel an earthquake during the movie?" I ask.

Vinny ponders. "Yeah, last time we came here, there was an earthquake."

Piper checks his phone. "Ok, Cindy, I hate to admit it, but you were right. We had an earthquake. It was a 6 magnitude."

"Must have been far away. My guardian angel kept us safe," Vinny says.

Piper looks up from his phone. "They're having another memorial service online."

"Again? When?" asks Vinny.

"Last Saturday this month," Piper says.

"I'm neva goin' there. Eva again," Stella said. "It's bad luck."

Dear Diary,

Mooresville was hit again. Some buildings are ruined. A local firetruck disappeared. They found it in Virginia. I have to figure this out. I need answers. Why do people around here care more about a firetruck than mega rocks falling in the sky? We had another earthquake. Michigan got another bad hit. Seems like this is World War III against asteroids. Virtual memorial services cannot be the new way of life.

Cindy's Bedroom May 2054

I look up at my ceiling. I feel different about windows now. My lamp is looking nice. It works. Somehow it gives me a new sense of peace. *My lamp. I love my lamp.*

Dear Diary,

My neighbor gave me a new lightbulb. The safe kind. He is nice. Noah. He didn't make fun of my hair. I don't want to remember what else happened today. I was home alone when our front window exploded. What the heck!

2

MUDFLAT GARDEN

Cindy's World Thursday, August 13, 2054

Strange things are happening. They still haven't figured out who stole the firetruck. *Who cares about the firetruck! Could someone please think about saving birds and animals and, I don't know, how about...people? Could someone please care about saving people? How can it ever be the same? Flying rocks are changing the Earth. What is this world coming to?*

At any moment, the fourth meteor strike is going to hit North and South America. Ever since the third strike in

May, I struggle with doubts about where I am going to college and what I am doing with my life. Forget about deciding on a major. The third strike has caused the most damage, injuring half of the people on Earth. I'm stressed out all the time and can't seem to snap out of it. For those who still care about life, we are all thinking it: *Will I survive the next strike?*

We are on the west side of North Carolina. It's my first time going to the mudflats to see a race. Trucks will be spinning and sliding at the Mud Slide Bonanza. The reason why I am going is because my brother is racing in it. It might help me keep my mind off the strikes. After the great world misfortune hit in May, I am trying to stay away from gloomy and narrow reflections. I hope I don't have another panic attack.

It's Piper's first time, too. He never assures me of my safety because his focus is on a successful outcome. His feeling of enthusiasm and determination is contagious. "Cindy, try to have some fun! And don't waste your time reading sad trash."

"This isn't sad! And it isn't trash! It's a really good story. The main character is a hero. He stays really calm while his planet is falling apart." I continue to read my book with a high level of determination to finish it. When I am done, I just might read another book from this author. He seems to know the secrets of nature.

Can my brother really pull this off—win the purse and drive away with his Jeep undamaged? He's rather ambitious. Ouch! That hurt. I look at my finger and see a paper cut. I fold the corner of the page I had been reading and set my book next to my left leg in the passenger seat. I'm almost finished with it, *Freedom In Another Galaxy*. Piper drives his white Jeep Wrangler into the parking lot and looks for Vinny.

A black Jeep pulls into a parking spot. It's Piper's best friend, Vinny. Growing up in a poor family, Vinny began working at a young age. Vinny was in a terrible car accident in high school and almost died. He went through a miraculous change and insists he has a guardian angel. Piper steps over to greet his racing buddy and Stella. The couple gets out of Vinny's Jeep. She is the same ole Stella I met at the movie theater last spring when she was with Vinny.

"Vinny!" she cries out larger than life in the parking lot. "My ticket!"

Vinny reaches into his pocket, hands her a little paper stub, and looks proud. "Don't say I neva' did nothin'."

Piper and Vinny get in their vehicles and enter through the gate as racers. Stella and I head to the entrance as spectators. I see a private entrance for people who live at Mudflat Garden Estates.

Someone near the entrance is lifting his arm in the air and repeating something. He is holding a small piece of paper in his hand and yelling. "Jesus saves!"

"What a nice surprise, Linda. Vinny neva said nothin about you comin' along with Pipa. I came out ta see the *mystery ship* everyone's talkin' about. You know, it just happened to show up in the mud. I mean, how'd it do that? I've got to see it with my own eyes to believe it."

I love her New York accent.

"I wonder how it got there." It's hard for me to understand how a ship just showed up in a muddy place.

It's been in the news non-stop ever since the third meteor strike. Storms make certain trees fall, which I find completely unnatural, but this ship is out of place. It is more unnatural than the firetruck. Most surprisingly of all, over 7,500 satellites in Earth's atmosphere are still working.

"It's nice keeping in touch with you. I thought Piper was nuts when he registered for a mud race. Yesterday, he invited me to come along. It was a last-minute thing. You know, the third strike…it really shook me up."

"Hey girl, it shook everyone up, even the whole planet."

I look for Piper's Jeep. I'm impressed with his perseverance, passion, and goals, even if he has no interest in joining our father's motorcycle business. These qualities are missing in my life. Recently, this race has become the most important event to him. He is hoping to win and use the money from this race to finish shooting his Hitchcock style movie. My only determination, passion, and goal, as far as I can tell, apply to finishing a good book.

What am I doing here? I should have stayed back home where I could be drinking sweet tea and reading my book in my comfortable chair. Why is this mystery ship so important? Can't someone figure out how to stop the next meteor strike due to hit Earth at any moment?

People crowd around at the entrance. There are all kinds of signs sticking up from the ground on wood sticks. NO GLASS BOTTLES. GATES OPEN AT 8AM. TRUCKS ONLY. NO DIRTBIKES. NO ATVS. GOLF CARTS WELCOME ON TRAILS ONLY. CAMPING FRI & SAT NIGHT. NO PETS. ENTER AT YOUR OWN RISK. FIRES IN BARRELS ONLY. NO THROWING ROCKS. NO FIGHTING. SPECTATORS MUST STAY BEHIND

THE FENCE. SPINNING IN MUD PITS ONLY. VIOLATORS WILL BE REMOVED. It would be devastating if a meteor strike hit this location again because this race has so many people. The people counter at the entrance reads over 100,000 people have been killed in the USA, a big number for a dwindling population.

As a *walk-up*, I see how much it costs to get in. Since, it had been a last-minute decision to go to the races, I missed the early bird discount of twenty tokens. A lady behind the counter scans twenty-five tokens from my electronic wallet, hands me a map, and tells me to have a good time. Not knowing what to expect, I doubt that I will have a good time. What could be so fun about watching trucks drive 'round and 'round when half the world is gone? *Where did Stella go? Did I lose her?* I look around and see her standing by herself while she fidgets with her map.

"Linda…" Stella takes a quick glance to notice I am standing with her. She squints as she brings the map closer to her. Then she looks back at me. "Why do they have to make it so difficult? It doesn't even say where ta go!"

"It's Cylinda, not Linda."

"Yeah. Well, you know. I'm terrible with names. It sounds like *Linda*, and you sort'a look like a *Linda*." Her tone is husky and confident.

"Well, it's *Cylinda*. Sort of like Cinderella." I open up my map to find the nearest restroom. "My mom wanted to name me Cinderella, but my dad wouldn't go for it. He thought I'd get teased, and people would ask to see my glass slippers, so they settled on Cylinda. You can call me Cindy. My dad calls me Cylinda. My mom calls me Cinderella."

"Cinderella—kinda catchy. I like it. Why would anyone tease *you*? You'd neva hurt a flea."

"Never mind." I don't think it is necessary to refer to the glass slipper, so I change the subject. "I've never been to a mud race before."

"Me eith'a. Piper made you pay? Ugh!" She gave me a friendly slug in my left shoulder. "Tsa! Don't let him get away with it."

Ow! That really hurt! I rub it out to get rid of the pain.

A couple of teenage boys walk by and smirk. "You girls lost already?"

"Oh, get a life." Stella's natural tendency was defensiveness. "Go both'a someone else." If there is one thing Stella could do, she could stick up for herself.

24

"I don't mind paying for my own ticket." I look up from the map. "I don't want to feel like I owe Piper anything."

"Well, don't give him any gas money, girlfriend. Where do we go, anyway?"

"This place is big! It looks like the track for the first round is this one. We go that way." I point to the left.

The rocks can fall anywhere. I try not to think about falling rocks. Maybe it's safe here. Gryffonland Amusement Park was ruined by the third meteor strike in May.

"Looks like the mystery ship is over by the first track. It's that way. Let's go to the Sticky Stand. I need to use the restroom first."

Stella decides she is also going to empty her *bladdah*. There is a poster on the inside stall door with a big picture of a butterfly. It's a beautiful Eastern-tailed Blue Butterfly. After relieving myself, I walk over to wash my hands. The automatic soap dispenser spits a light brown substance in my hand. When I place my hands under the faucet, water streams out automatically. The soap begins to feel slippery as I mix it around on my palms. *What is this muddy soap? Hmm.* I rinse my hands and while I am drying them with a paper towel, I notice a poster hanging on the wall: FROGS! DONATE TODAY! *Look at how many animals are endangered!*

How do we know what they're going to do with the money? "How do they know all these animals are endangered?"

"They research it, girlfriend." Stella dries her hands while standing next to me. She speaks confidently as if she has the frog situation figured out.

Her arms are moving, and it makes me think about protecting my shoulder. I step away in case she decides to give me another one of her friendly slugs.

"Awe. They're so cute." Stella likes the frog poster.

I notice big black bulging eyes and a shiny wet nose designed on the poster. It is not possible for me to imagine the frog as *cute*. "Cute?"

"Someone's gotta save 'em. I'll give em' a token. Where do we go to donate?"

"Oh, look. It says the St. Francis Butterfly is endangered. They take donations at the Mud Market." I check my paper cut again, and I notice it is healed up. *Hmm. That was quick.* I throw the paper towel in the trash can and notice a poster advertising bars of healing brown soap.

When we arrive at the Sticky Stand, which is nothing more than the type of metal bleachers at a high school football game, Stella shows great enthusiasm to see that the last two seats available are in the front row.

Stella draws closer to me, speaking as if she has to keep it a secret from the rest of the world. "How lucky can we get? The best seats in the house, huh?"

The mystery ship is sitting right in the middle of the track! Looks like she's right—maybe these seats are the best ones. *How in the world did the ship get there?* Stella plops right down and makes herself at home as if she could blend right in with the crowd. I notice how Stella never talks about the meteor strikes. Maybe she's uncomfortable about it because it's beyond her control. She probably just wants to ignore it.

There is a piece of paper sitting on my seat. I pick up the paper and read the front. It says, "Four Spiritual Laws." It must be what the guy at the entrance was handing out. I sit down feeling like I am taking someone else's seat. Unsure that we will be able to stay in the front row, I sit on the paper. I keep my purse close in my lap and feel unsettled. "Maybe someone else is sitting here, and we're taking their seats."

"We're not givin' up these seats." Stella means it, speaking in a determined way with her confident reasoning. She speaks softly so that no one can hear but me. "There's nowhere else ta go. So don't even think about it. If someone tries to kick us out, don't even budge. They's gotta be the ones ta go find anotha' seat. Not us." Her eyebrows shot up when she put an emphasis on the word *they's*.

Stella tells me she is the daughter of an Italian doctor who specializes in sports medicine. She moved with her family from the Big Apple to live in a charming southern 'burb near Charlotte, North Carolina. She is a people-person who sells kitchen products and hosts monthly parties at other people's houses. She loves being the center of attention. She always wants to be right, and I discover she has savvy business skills, which includes, of course, getting free stuff.

Stella and I are different. She is excited to see all the trucks, but I only have an interest in making it home safe. She stands out like a New York Met on the Brave's baseball field in Atlanta, Georgia, while I feel like I blend right in with the crowd.

The mystery ship makes me curious and since the park is well landscaped, I feel somewhat comfortable to be waiting for round one to start any minute. Still, I feel like a square peg in a round hole. I can't help but sit here and think about my purpose in life. I decide right now that I am not going to sell kitchen stuff.

Who am I? I can't just be the lady-who-is-sitting-with-the-kitchen-lady. What is the meaning of life anyway? What is going on in the world?

3

THE RACE

Cindy's World

I hear a drum roll over a loudspeaker and upbeat, energetic music begins. Someone in the crowd whistles when two metal doors swing open, and the trucks begin to enter at low speed. The audience stands and cheers as they applaud. My feet feel the metal stands rumble.

The first truck drives right by our section and the audience roars. Strawberry Punch is in a red Chevy Silverado, propped up higher than usual, showing off big tires and shiny wheels. The next racer named Green

Machine is in a Ford truck, camouflaged by a green, black, and khaki paint job, dressed in big tires and black wheels. With a limit of thirty trucks in the first round, they drive by one at a time. Grease Lightning waves out the window of a dark gray truck with silver lightning painted down the side. The trucks follow one another to a waiting location where they park on the front side of the track. Piper the Snowy Owl is fourth, and Vinny the Night Owl is fifth. Just as if they were lining up at a drive-through restaurant, thirty trucks park in a long row. I begin to wonder if any of the drivers get hurt. *How dangerous could it get?*

The spectators hear a man's voice on a loudspeaker. "Hi! I'm Ralph Timberlake. We'd like to welcome you to Mr. J's tenth mud racing event, the Mud Slide Bonanza! Please always remain behind the fence. We hope that you will become a member of the Mud Racing Jamboree while you are here, and you can do so when you stop by the Mud Market, which is where you will also be able to find a souvenir. The Mud Market is located directly next to this track. And in just a moment, we will hear the call to begin. Let's hear it from Mr. J's best fans in the world!"

The crowd cheers wildly.

I see a young boy sitting next to me.

"Have you been here before?" I ask.

"This is my fifth year! Have you been here before?" He smiles, looking delighted to be sitting in the front row, fully engaged with the race and so are his buddies. The boys must be about ten or eleven years old.

I speak loud to him over the music while the trucks exit to the left. "This is my first time!"

"You must be real serious to sit in the front row!" The friendly boy smiles again and laughs. I can't hear him very well. "The racers are supposed to stay under one minute." He points to a digital clock, and then we watch the last truck follow the others. "What is your name?"

"Cindy," I say. "What's yours?"

"Danny!"

A female voice interjects on the loud intercom. "Once the race begins, we won't stop! Drivers, are you ready?"

A male's voice is heard next. "On your mark, get set, let the race begin!" I hear a gunshot. Strawberry Punch peels out from the starting line on the back left side of the track, traveling clockwise. The trucks race one at a time against the clock.

The boy next to me whispers something to his two buddies. They point at me and laugh.

"What's so funny?" I suddenly feel as if they know something that I don't know.

He says something, but I can't hear. It sounds like he might have said the number *five*.

I want to know what he said. "What?"

He points to the digital clock. He and his two buddies seem enthusiastic about the surroundings, thrilled to have a good view, and squirm on the edge of their seats.

I look at the digital clock and see the numbers turning. The red truck speeds up a ramp, flies in the air, and lands in the mud. Then it travels in a clockwise direction at full speed and turns, sort of sideways, when going around the bend.

A boy yells to the boy next to me. "Danny! Eighteen!"

Eighteen? Why is he saying eighteen? Here comes the red truck. It's going to pass by. It is so loud! Oh no, it's coming close to the fence right in front of us! Is it going to hit the fence?

"Twenty-five!" The boys cheer and yell.

As the truck makes a sliding right-hand turn and passes by our section, it surprisingly flings a huge amount of mud up into the air. There is no time to move. I can hardly believe what is happening. Mud flies directly at us!

I had no idea! What did we get ourselves into?

It all happened too fast. Stella and I have blotches of mud on us—a glob of mud on my shirt, another glob of mud on my pants. Mud on one foot and on one metallic copper water-friendly sandal. Even mud on one side of my purse.

"Are you kiddin' me?" Stella looks shocked and angry at first. She happened to get more mud on her than I did. "I need to get me one of them pieces of cardboard."

I see the boy next to me and his buddies are scrunched down on the floor, hunching in a ball as low as they could get. The boys pop up and point at us, laughing hysterically. They jump up and down with great excitement. I'm speechless, sitting in a new outfit, decorated in mud.

"Get ready for the next one," the boy yells out.

I look at Stella, and she looks at me.

"I had no idea. Did you?" I say.

She hardly shakes her head no, and all we can do is laugh.

The next gunshot goes off, and I see Green Machine going up the ramp. I look behind me and see spectators with a piece of cardboard that reads ROUND ONE: THIRTY TRUCKS.

Thirty trucks! Why didn't I notice the sign before?

There is no time to hide. The camouflaged Ford takes a big sideways spin when it makes a long right-hand turn, flinging even more mud up into the air. I am a little more prepared this time, covering my face while hoping the truck doesn't slam into the fence. A big glob of mud lands in my hair.

Stella calls out to a worker in the stand. "Hey! Excuse me! We need two of those!"

The worker glances her way and happens to know what Stella wants even though he is far away.

"You gotta duck when the truck comes around." The boy's words of wisdom speak a little too late.

"Oh, I see. You duck when the clock says twenty-five. Right. I get it now." I notice the next truck ready to peel out.

The third gunshot went off.

Here we go again. This is going too fast!

"Haven't you ever been to Seawater Aquapark?" the boy asks me. "We saw the dolphin show! I sat in the front row and got drenched!"

There is no time to think about his question because I am looking for cardboard. Stella is desperately waiting for the worker to make his way over to us. Greased Lightning takes a lop-sided landing off the ramp. It lands on the back right tire and then on the front right tire.

"Do you always sit in the front row?" I ask the boy to my left.

"It's the only way to go!" He smiles.

Stella becomes impatient, stands up, and reaches out her arm. "Hurry up! I NEED TWO OF THOSE!"

A person yells from behind. "Hey, excuse me, miss! You need to sit down!"

The worker stumbles over to Stella the best he can and places two cardboard signs in Stella's hands.

Stella hands me a sign, and we see the clock turn twenty-five. *Oh no! The third truck is getting too close to us! Is it going to hit the fence?* I hold the cardboard up in front of my face. I hear a sliding squelch. *Splat!* A loud motor roars a fine tune and speeds to the finish line. This time, a glob of mud sticks onto the back of my shirt.

So it goes, on and on, where trucks are zooming off the ramp, sliding into a right-hand corner U-turn at full speed ahead, and sliding way too close to our section while mud flies up in the air. I see Piper and Vinny and all the rest of the trucks race right by us. Finally, fifteen winners from round one are announced. The crowd walks away perplexed when the announcer makes a final announcement. In an attempt to satisfy everyone's curiosity, Ralph Timberlake reveals how the mystery ship had arrived during the third strike.

"A quantum leap?" I try hard to imagine a ship teleporting. It can't be possible. There must be another explanation.

"Who would'a eva thought that Vinny and Pipa would make it to round two?" Stella is proud of her man.

I suddenly want to learn more about the ship. "Did you hear what that guy just said?"

"Neva gunna get me ta know about physics," Stella says. "But if that's what they say, then that's what they say."

No wonder why so many people flocked to this mud race. They really want to see the ship. Maybe some of the news reports were correct. Maybe some of the strange things that have been happening relate to a quantum leap. Other reports say it is some type of annihilation. "Do people really think that the ship was in the ocean one minute, and the next minute it's in the mudflats? That's crazy!"

"I know. Right? Don't believe everything you hear." Sometimes Stella sounds like a recorder, spitting back information that someone else had told her, but acting as if she's speaking for herself.

"How do you think it got there?"

"Beats me. I'm not goin' anywhere near that thing. Ya might end up in the Bermuda Triangle. Maybe we oughta walk around with a life jacket, just in case." Stella laughs at her joke, and I laugh along.

"So, no one can go in the mystery ship."

"Nope. Must be haunted. Gotta be. It gives me the creeps. Look at it. But the otha' ship, the Dreamboat, now that one's gunna be impressive."

"The what-boat?"

"Don't cha watch the news? The space force put it togetha' in three months. It can hold like 10,000 people. It's a whole city. Amazing. You can stay the night in it."

"Oh, yeah. Sounds familiar. Strange, isn't it—a space force making a cruise ship? What's it called? It's the cruise-ship-sitting-on-dry-ground. I heard about it."

"It's called the Galaxy Dreamboat. And you know what they say?"

"What?"

"At any second, it's going to end up in the ocean. That's why it's sold out. People want to go for a ride in it."

"But there's no water!" Suddenly, I want to do a search on my phone.

I tap on my screen. It says here that the Galaxy Dreamboat was built in this place, Mudflat Garden Acres. I hope I make it out of this place alive because my book is waiting for me in Piper's Jeep.

4

THE NAVAL SHIP

Cindy's World

There must be some other explanation for how the so-called *mystery ship* arrived. Some people are saying it is a hoax for the mud race to make more money. Maybe they are right. It is interesting to see a navy ship positioned at a racetrack, most definitely yes, as if someone deliberately chose to place it there. I get my phone and do a quick search.

A report here says, "Soon after the third strike hit in May, a hiker went out to explore, and he found what the news first called a mystery ship. After the vessel was discovered, Ralph Timberland built a mud track around it.

The United States Historic Ship Organization (USHSO) insists that someone stole the ship."

There's no such thing as aliens, right?

Since Mr. J's event travels around, they chose to have the race in this location on purpose, no doubt. I am leaning toward believing that the transplant is some type of a prank. I don't think the United States government would lie about such an unusual type of theft. If someone did steal the ship, how did they get it all the way out to the middle of nowhere?

I observe the land surrounding the ship. There is a crevice so large that the ship could fit in it, but it is blocked off for safety. Although the vessel is leaning to the side at a small angle, it would be possible to walk on the deck. Running might be more difficult. It looks unstable enough to keep away from venturing too close. Fitting down snug into the ground, the vessel is surrounded by a sea of mud and blocked off by large cement blocks.

I see where I can get a brochure to learn more about the status of this naval ship. Stella and I walk towards a female worker who is handing out brochures. The worker hands me a free brochure, and I take a look.

"Hang on. I want to read this."

"What does it say?" Stella asks.

THE USS NORTH CAROLINA (BB-55)

Once located at the North Carolina Battleship Memorial,
this "Showboat" has relocated from Wilmington, NC,
to the mudflats of western NC.
Before discovering the new location of the ship,
the citizens of Wilmington, NC, became quite upset
and claimed that this ship had been taken away
without any approval by the USHSO.
After the ship was found, it was determined that
it is too heavy to bring back to the original
National Historic Landmark site.
It remains in the current location while there is an investigation.
At this time, the ship has been determined as dangerous,
due to the slanted position, and it is not open to the public.
The USHSO hopes that this ship will continue to be
a major tourist attraction.
Thank you for vising Mr. J's mud race event,
and thank you for viewing the USS North Carolina.

"It must be some kind of a publicity stunt." Stella quickly makes up her mind.

"Maybe. Maybe that's what they want you to think."

"Well, if that's what they say, then that's what they say."

"Who's they," I ask.

"I don't know."

We laugh.

We walk by a journalist from Channel 9 News. She is about to report live in front of a camera. Stella and I wait to hear her speak into a microphone.

"Larry, I'm standing here outside the first mud race, located northwest of the city of Statesville in the state of North Carolina. Members and non-members from Mr. J's 10th annual mud race event have seen the mystery ship up close for the first time. This is the first time it has been available to the public since it was discovered in a new location, although citizens are not allowed to go on board. This mystery ship has been identified as the *USS North Carolina* and confirmed as a naval ship from World War II. The *United States Historic Ship Organization* has confirmed that this ship is not something from outer space, and aliens did not make it.

"This ship appears to be the same ship that is missing from Wilmington, North Carolina, although there are some disputes as to whether or not this is the same exact ship. It now sits at a slant, part way down inside the Earth's crust. You might be pleased to find out that an announcement has been made by Mr. J's owner, Ralph Timberland, after the first race finished. Earlier today, he stated that the way this naval ship arrived must have been by what he calls a quantum leap. He is very much open to returning this ship to Wilmington, but no one knows how to get it back. There is some debate as to what the *quantum leap* means exactly, so we are waiting to find out. A press conference is scheduled for later this afternoon. Larry, back to you."

My mind thinks I'd like to get to the bottom of this issue, although Stella seems not to be in the least bit interested. Her approach seems to be from the view of a tourist, while my curiosity is packed with questions.

I see golf carts moving down a path one at a time, and the drivers make us wait to cross over to the other side. I see one cart has black leather seats. Two adults in the front. Two kids in the back all buckled in. I know Stella wants to ride in a golf cart by the way she looks at them, as if something is on the tip of her tongue. If she could make someone slam on their breaks, she probably would. It's a matter of time before Stella either sticks out her thumb or waves someone down.

I'd rather not beg for a ride. I really don't mind walking. I step aside to avoid another one of her friendly slugs.

There is a curiosity inside of me I can't get away from. I want to find out more about the naval ship.

***

All this reminds me of my early days when a lost dog showed up in our neighborhood. Some of the neighbors wanted to keep the cute, fluffy dog, while other neighbors wanted to find its owner. Still, other neighbors could care less. Me, on the other hand, I put some thought into why and how the dog escaped. Janie, my next-door neighbor, called the number on the dog tag right away. We waited for the owner to drive over and pick up his pet. When the owner finally arrived, Janie seemed eager to return the dog. There was a small crowd of neighbor kids wanting to see the owner, but they didn't want to talk to him. The situation remained pleasant and friendly at first. The owner smiled, scooped up his fluffy white dog, said *thank you* to Janie, and then I had to ask.

"How did your dog get out?" I thought my question was innocent, but it must have made the mouthy neighbor boy, Eddie, think of his next verbal attack.

"Oh," the owner searched for an answer. "We must have left the gate open."

Eddie blurted out rudely. "Your dog could have got run over by a car, you know!" His boisterous comment offended the owner.

"Mind your own business!" the owner snapped, marching away quickly. He placed his dog in the back seat of his car and drove away.

At the time, I thought I was responsible for Eddie suddenly becoming brave enough to shoot his mouth off. After all, the situation had been friendly until I asked the first question.

Similar situations come up year after year, and it makes me silent my questions. I prefer peace over chaos. I prefer friendliness over hostility. My mind continues to race with questions. If there is one person who would stay up all night to figure out how to untie the Gordian Knot, it's me, Cindy Smith.

How did the USS North Carolina relocate? What kind of a person believes in a quantum leap anyway? Did Albert Einstein believe in things like this? Maybe somehow, I will find out.

5

THE MUD MARKET

Cindy's World

I begin walking on the path while Stella finishes eyeballing another golf cart. It slowly passes by. The cart is holding six people, and there is not enough room for us to hop in.

My khaki shorts aren't dark enough to blend in with the mud blotch on my left side. The strap of my black flat leather purse hangs on my right shoulder and drapes across to the left side of my hip. It holds my driver's license, cherry lip balm, a map, brochure, my phone, and the "Jesus Saves" paper. We walk at a brisk pace, fast enough to keep moving, and it suddenly feels like we are power walking with the rest of the crowd. We pass by a couple of slow walkers as Stella tells me more about her kitchen parties.

"So, Nancy has almost twenty people on her guest list. That's pretty good."

"When is your next party?"

"Next Friday. Nancy lives off Brawley School Road, and she invited some of her neighbors. I book the parties on Fridays and Saturdays. You know, it's the best time ta' get the biggest crowd."

"Of course. You know, I heard a big meteorite touched down in that area."

"Yeah, they got a bad one, Nancy said. It's too bad. A kitchen party is a good way to see who's left out there. You know, it's a good time to try and get some people togetha'."

"It's hard to imagine half the world population is gone."

Stella says nothing.

I find it strange that something so bizarre is happening in the world but some people, like Stella for instance, are more comfortable ignoring it. She seems oblivious to the fact that a meteorite could strike at any moment since the August meteor shower began a few days ago and has been going non-stop, landing in random spots on each continent. Some of the asteroids have broken through the Earth's atmosphere. Some of them burn up as falling stars, but others have been touching down as meteorites. There are too many to pinpoint which ones will land and which ones will burn up.

We keep walking until we get to the Mud Market. The prized market is spread out. I see a fresh farmer's market covered by a large white tent overhang. There are apples, oranges, melons, grapes, and several other fruits and vegetables mixed in with camping items such as knitted hot pad holders, tongs, can openers, and hand-woven baskets. "Twenty-five tokens for a cantaloupe?"

"It feeds a lot of people," says Stella, figuring it all out.

Beyond the farmer's market, there is a wonderful aroma coming from an outdoor grill where picnic tables are set. I see a private building tucked away, off the path, and I assume it might be for tools, tractors, and storage.

"Mmm-mmm! Chicken on the grill!" Stella is a fan of barbeques.

I see another building with a sign that reads, MUDDY SOUVENIRS. Another building has a sign that says MUDFLAT GARDEN WINERY.

"I'm going to pick out a souvenir when we head back." It's no fun carrying around extra weight and needing to keep track of it the rest of the day.

I follow Stella over to the outdoor grill for lunch. The entrees look like something from a Robby Jay show: Tuscan Rosemary Smoked Whole Chickens, Texas-Style Brisket, Beer-Simmered Bratwurst, Glazed Chicken Thighs, Smoked Prime Rib, and Grilled Steak. No wonder the smell is delicious. I look around to see if I can find Robby the smiling chef, but it is highly unlikely. I see three men wearing tall white chef hats standing behind the long table. I'm embarrassed to ask the Iron Chef if they have any vegetarian kabobs. Stella and I stand in a short line leading to an outdoor buffet.

When it is my turn, I pay the cashier seven tokens for a one-trip-through BBQ lunch and wonder how many people pay ten tokens for an all-you-can eat meal. Some things in America never change. Stella selects the glazed chicken breast, macaroni, breadsticks, and green beans, placing them on a sturdy paper plate. I select the veggie kabobs, yellow rice, and strawberry Jell-o. Next to the brisket sitting under a red heat lamp, we take a fork and a napkin at the end of the line. At another table, Stella pours fresh squeezed lemonade into a paper cup while I pour myself a cup of sweet tea.

Stella looks for the cleanest spot and sits. She doesn't ask me if I am comfortable with the seat she selected. I follow her and sit. The first half of our meal is peaceful. Stella continues to tell me about her kitchen parties and the free gifts she will offer at Nancy's house.

Two men sit not too far from us, and I recognize them as maintenance workers from the park. Stella squints her eyes and looks at them suspiciously, which makes her quiet for only a couple of moments.

"I neva did like that kind of a jumpsuit," Stella leans in, talking softly. "Looks like they should be in jail or somethin'. Look how baggy it is. They could almost hide a kid inside, and no one would eva know."

I sit still and hope no one can hear her. I see one of the workers lift a heavy work boot and step over the bench. He lifts the other big bulky boot over the bench and sits down to eat with his friend. I notice another paper on the table. I wonder what it says on the back. I turn it over. "Oh, look what I found, 'The Four Spiritual Laws.' Law one says you are loved. God loves you, and He has good plans for you."

"The big guy in the sky has it all." Stella says confidently.

"Excuse me?" A thin woman is looking for a place to sit. She is carrying her lunch and stops when she sees the two workers in a jumpsuit. She speaks loud enough for us to hear. "Do you work here?"

"You think?" One of the workers grins while the other one lets out a chuckle. "You want something?"

"Do you know anything about the mystery ship? I mean, like, how did it get here all the way from Wilmington?"

"Did you hear Ralph Timberlake?"

"Yes. I heard what he said. You really think people are going to buy into that? There's no such thing as a quantum leap. It's made up. It's a figure of speech. The ship's a publicity stunt, right? Or are you going to tell me it'll be a myth? It must be a political move. I mean, is the government working with this mud race?"

"What are you a news reporter?" The men chuckle at the same time. "Watch Channel 9 News tonight, miss, or do a search on the Internet. You might find something."

"I just thought you might know something. Do you work on the ship?"

"We take care of the grounds. That's about it." The man sounds as if he's smart enough to do much more. "Now how about you suddenly disappear from this table and suddenly appear at that table? Then come back and tell me how you did it."

The two men chuckle again.

The woman sees that they are teasing her. She gives up talking to them. As she moves away from them, unsatisfied with the outcome of the conversation, she huffs. She walks closer to us and stands next to Stella. "Is anyone sitting here?"

"Nope." Stella answers with a friendly look in her eye. I bet she's hoping to meet a new friend who will book a party.

I glance at the two male workers. My questions are bubbling inside of me. I admire the way this woman came right out and spoke what is on most everyone's mind. "I heard what you said over there. So, how do you think the ship got there?"

"Who knows? Maybe a UFO picked it up. Then they decided they didn't want a big piece of metal. Maybe aliens forgot where they found it, and so they had to dump it somewhere." The woman spoke with dry humor, and she did not smile.

I couldn't help but get the impression that she was annoyed by the fact that it is impossible to disappear and reappear, which is exactly what Ralph Timberland from the mud races want his race fans to believe. Part of me could see the woman getting so obnoxious to the point that she'd get kicked out of the park, and I didn't want to get wrapped up in that kind of a mess.

It was a lot of maybes, but I played along. "So, why would a UFO want to pick it up in the first place?"

"How would I know? I'm not an alien. Go ask an alien, and when you find one, let me know what they say." Clearly, the lady had made fun of the UFO theory. Still, I like her inquisitive nature. At least she is willing to talk about it, unlike Stella who seems to keep her lips pressed on the issue.

Stella buts in. "Oh, the chicken looks really good, doesn't it?"

"I don't eat chicken that much." I feel content with my veggie kabobs.

"Law Two: eat more chicken."

"Let's see...Law Two says today is a new day. We all fall short of God's perfect standard of divine holiness. We need to confess this brokenness with a humble heart."

Stella drinks her lemonade. "Eat more chicken is a good law, right? Betta' be nice to the big guy in the sky 'cause He made all the chicken. Listen, we're not gunna figure out a quantum leap sittin' here. People like Einstein know how to do physics. They'll figure it out. It is what it is, and ya know what? Let's leave the mystery ship to smart people. Now let's enjoy our lunch. I wanna go see the cruise ship. Who knows? I might even make a reservation and stay the night on it."

"It's sold out, sister," the woman replied in a nippy tone. She changed her demeanor quickly. "Better luck next time."

Seems like she is perturbed that Stella said we are not going to figure out a quantum leap. I could feel myself rising to the occasion of telling Stella to speak for herself. Stella really shouldn't say we're not smart people.

The woman takes a drink and is more than ready to challenge Stella's statement. "Maybe you're not going to figure it out, but maybe I will."

A young man walks over. He seems to have a calming effect on her because her face softened, she let out a small sigh, and her shoulders relaxed when she saw him.

"There's my new wife! Narissa," he says, "where are the drinks?"

"Right over there, babe."

It is quiet at the table for a moment while Stella is ignoring Narissa's offensive comment.

"Law Three: Book a kitchen party and get free gifts." Stella says, changing the subject.

"Let's see. Law three says you matter. God wants a personal relationship with you because you matter to Him." I look up and see Narissa's husband drink from his glass of lemonade.

"I told ya. The big guy in the sky wants to give you a bunch of free stuff," Stella says.

The couple sits in a romantic cloud of flirty looks and silent smiles between the two of them.

"Get this," Narissa points to the maintenance workers. "See those two guys over there?"

"Yeah. So?" Her husband does not seem interested.

"They work on the cruise ship, and one of 'em has a nametag that says, Shipmate Catfish. And get this. He's one of the janitors."

"Catfish? What a name. I doubt his mother named him that."

"Catfish the janitor." Narissa giggles, and the rest of lunch goes well.

6

CALVIN KING

Calvin's World

A tour guide is walking down a long hall. His shiny black shoes are silently stepping on dark purple carpet lined with large geometrically shaped yellow stars. The bottom half of the walls are covered with dark gray wallpaper blasted with millions of silvery white stars, trimmed in bright yellow molding. The young man walks past an open door to a private meeting room. Located on the other side of the hallway, oddly enough, the wall includes special reinforced glass. Plans for the Galaxy Dreamboat started well over two years ago, and most of the assembly had finished before the strikes began.

"King!" a voice yells from inside a private room. The voice is from the cruise ship captain.

The tour guide in the hallway stops, turns around, and leans his head into the room. "Captain?"

"How is it with you?"

"I'm taking the next group in five minutes. What's up?" Calvin asks.

The captain looks up from a piece of paper. "Did you check the weather report?"

"Not recently. No."

"Crikey! The next storm is due to hit in this location."

"Meteors? When?"

"In about thirty minutes." The captain's voice speaks with authority.

"How long will this one last?"

"Check the report before going on duty. Check it or I'll crack you like a flea. The storm will last about an hour. Looks like it'll be on and off for the whole afternoon, and then it'll die down around five. Where's your flashlight?"

"I don't have it. Sir, with all due respect, it's mid-afternoon. The sun is high up in the sky. Is the second race cancelled?"

"No. Not that I know of."

"Should I still take them to the upper deck, Captain?"

"They want to see the show. That's what we're here for, isn't it—to see the show? You know the bottom line. I will leave it up to you. I can't force you to go, but if you don't, I'll feed you to the sharks. So off you go."

"Captain, will any of the falling stars touch down? Your opinion, Sir." The tour guide remains factual.

"Check the report on your app. That's what it's there for."

"Captain, the truth, Sir. If I'm going to take a group of people up there, I need to be sure about what I'm getting into."

"Don't give me that bilge. We've been through this before. All maritime protocols and safety regulations will be strictly followed, or I'll peel your skin like a mango. Have everyone sit down in the chairs, and you'll see flashes in the northeast. Go over the rules. Earlier today, we had some swag-bellied wisecrack step his foot over the line, and he was made to walk the plank."

"Sir, security made him leave."

Captain Sam Bellamy raised his eyebrows. "Let it be a lesson."

"Maritime, Captain? We're on dry land."

"Bend your ear to this. There's no time for comedy when a meteor hits. This is still a ship. You will follow the ship's security plan and procedures for stowaways, refugees, hijackers, pirates, and terrorist threats. Keep guests out of restricted areas. For certain, I'm not sending you out into a war zone. I wouldn't send you up there if I knew the sky was falling. You're a space force tour guide, not a jungle boat comedian. So by all that is great and good, get out there and find your group. I'll be in the lobby greeting the guests."

"Yes, Captain." Calvin slightly nods his head in the affirmative.

"Now go to your duties, and I'll be wishing you a very good day."

After being recognized as a loyal tour guide, happy Calvin heads down the narrow hall to the tour departure location, for he is now determined to see the light show. He walks with gratitude for having this job. More importantly to Calvin the staff holds him in high regard.

At Calvin's previous place of employment, he was a captain on the Jungle Cruise at Gryffonland Amusement Park where he spent most of his waking hours outside. Now that he has a new job, he takes it quite seriously. It has been made known to the Dreamboat staff that he is one of the survivors from Michigan's meteor storm in May.

The next tour group shows their wristband and passes through the official gate. Calvin greets his next tour group as he usually does with great enthusiasm. "Hi, I'm Calvin, your guide for this tour. If you have any questions, please ask. It's my job to answer them. I spend all my time talking about this cruise ship."

He takes them down a narrow hallway until they reach the first restaurant, the Seahorse Cafe. He stops to tell them about the items on the menu, a variety of seafood, soft breads, cheeseburgers, pizza, and apple dishes. "The taco pizza is very popular."

Next, they walk by a few other small shops including the Dolphin Gift Shop, which is filled with souvenirs, books, and t-shirts. The gift shop is where childcare workers check in the children and adults sign up for badminton games. The dolphin mascot happens to be in the Soft Serve Ice Cream Shop where kids are getting a picture taken. Calvin takes the rest of the group down a bit further to the art gallery. "Just like Alice in Wonderland, you will discover more on this cruise ship than you have ever dreamed about. We will also be visiting the Upper Deck. If we're lucky, we might see a falling star up there today."

Knowing that he will not have enough time to tell the group about each piece of art, he paces himself to speak about his favorite selections. "This painting is one of my favorites, *La terrace de Sainte Adresse* by Claude Monet. Dated to 1867, it is a relaxing seascape showing three levels of sky, sea, and land. I am often tempted to sit in the chair."

The tour group laughs in unison to support his humor.

Calvin looks at his watch, and once the group passes by the art gallery, it is finally time to take the group to the top of the cruise ship. The first door to the upper deck is not labeled. It looks like a regular door with possibly nothing much behind it. Calvin announces to the group that once passing through the door, a waiver must be signed. Then he instructs the group to show their wristband and walk up the grand staircase.

He concludes with three simple rules. "Number one, stay behind the red line. Number two, remain seated in your chair when you are on the upper deck. And number three, anyone who does not follow the rules will be taken back downstairs where a crewman will escort you to walk the plank."

At the top of the grand staircase, a sign is posted on the second door. In a single file fashion, those from the tour group step through the doorway.

One woman, in particular, laughs out loud when she reads, ENTER AT YOUR OWN RISK.

A surfer has the need to explain himself for making his earlier comment. "We're under a falling star warning! Maybe this time I'll see a show!"

"You've been up there before?" a lady asks.

The surfer is eager to return. "This is my third time!"

7

WARNING

Cindy's World

Stella stands up. She seems eager to say good-bye to Narissa, the woman who sat next to us at lunch and didn't book a party. "Bye, Narissa."

I don't blame her. Narissa is a little rough around the edges when she speaks, almost as if at any minute she is going to drop her purse, spill out the contents, and start yelling. I can't tell if she always walks around like a basket case or if this seven-year crisis has a hold on her nerves, but either way, I don't really care to ask. A wise person once told me that a person can get to know another person in as little as forty-five minutes. While sitting at lunch, I learned a lot about Narissa. She had challenged the alien theory as well as the quantum leap theory, but she offered no other solution as to how the mystery ship traveled from Wilmington.

Before we leave the lunch table area, I take the map out of my purse and see where we need to go to get to the cruise ship. I open my map as I understand the value of this piece of paper. It's my lifeline for knowing how to get around. I see the direction we need to go and look up.

"We go that way." I point in the direction where many people are going.

Stella follows the people, almost blindly. She does not check her map.

I'm a little bit excited to see the cruise ship before the next mud race. My only hesitation stems from the idea that my first visit to a cruise ship should be at a real shipyard or a real port, not at one out in the middle of nowhere on dry ground. More questions begin to surface in my mind.

Why would our space force choose this location to build a cruise ship? They must have selected this desolate shipyard for a reason before the meteorite strikes even began. And since when is a space force in the business of building cruise ships? They're supposed to fly to Mars, not build luxury dreamboats. I wouldn't be surprised if the Galaxy Dreamboat is really an undercover warship. Who knows? Maybe it's something else altogether. I find myself becoming inquisitive again.

While we walk, I am discontented with the lack of knowledge about what is happening. Stella and I continue to walk in a hurry to stay on schedule. We need to be on time to Piper's next mud race. We have plenty of time, so I'm not too concerned. Despite the confusion surrounding the USS North Carolina, I see people enthusiastically approaching the Dreamboat. I hear one man suggest that the mystery ship might be a replica, and then another person says if it is a replica, then where did the original go? The conversation quickly returns to the alien theory.

We walk around a rolling hill and finally, I see the luxury cruise ship in the distance. It's breathtaking. Even from far away, the boat looks wonderfully magnificent. I hear many people *ooh* and *awe* at first sight once they see the amazing white vessel. It looks enormous. I imagine it must be bigger than the size of the ship that sank a long time ago, the *Titanic*. It looks to be about ten stories high. It is so wide that it makes the USS North Carolina look small. The oohing and aweing continue from behind me as I move closer to the ship with Stella.

"Mommy, mommy," a little girl is speaking. "Is the ship going to fly like the firetruck?"

"No, honey. Ships and firetrucks don't fly," her mother says. "Airplanes fly."

That ship is not flying anywhere.

It seems strange to see a ship sitting on dry ground. Somewhere close by, I hear a woman say that the ship might end up in the ocean one day. It seems impossible to think that the ocean could come this far inland. How in the world would that happen? I hear a woman behind us continue to speculate.

"It's possible that plates underneath the surface of the Earth can move apart. Remember the Pangea Theory where a supercontinent used to exist? It's possible that all the continents used to be connected. Some scientists say it's possible that it was a worldwide flood that tore the continents apart. If the continents used to be connected a long time ago, and then the one big continent spread apart when the plates shifted and split apart, who's to say the continents won't spread apart any further?"

A man who knows the woman speaks up. "Oh, Darla, you really believe that crap?"

Darla is quick to respond. "Why else would they build a cruise ship out in the middle of nowhere?"

"You really think it's a cruise ship?"

"What else would it be? What do you think it is? Look at it."

For a moment, it is silent.

"It's the Emerald City from the Wizard of Oz!" Someone calls out.

"No, it's a fish out of water!"

Someone laughs.

A man walks in our midst, listening to the public conversation. "Remember the story of Noah's Ark. Consider the rainbow. It's a promise that there won't be a worldwide flood ever again."

Then why did they build a...fish out of water?

Darla fires away. "But the earthquakes seem to be getting more frequent, and now we're in a seven-year meteor strike zone. There might not be a world-wide flood again, but it's proven that the plates have been shifting around quite a bit these days. It's possible that the plates could shift again, resulting in more continents. We could go from a world of seven continents to a world of twenty continents."

"Cindy!" A voice calls out from behind.

Someone knows my name? Who in the world could that be? No one ever remembers my name. I stop walking and turn around. Then Stella stops and turns around. I see a small group of boys running toward me with one boy leading the way.

"Cindy!"

I recognize the boy as the one who I sat next to at the mud race. He has dark sandy blond hair and greenish eyes. He runs right up to us with two friends following behind. All three boys have a firetruck toy in their hand, and they are making the firetrucks fly as they run.

"Speed of light!" One boy zooms his firetruck up and down in the air.

"Woooo!" The boy with freckles blasts a siren sound as he makes his firetruck fly.

"Oh, hello." I try to recall his name, and I remember it reminded me of a dandilion. My memory serves me well. When I met this boy at the first race, one of his friends had called him Danny-lion. I'm surprised that the boy became familiar with my name.

I can't imagine what this young boy wants to tell me, but it looks urgent. Did I drop something? I don't think so. Is he lost? It doesn't look like he is with a parent, and I never saw a parent sitting with them at the last race.

Stella does not seem to be interested in children.

"Are you going to the next mud race?" The boy is genuinely concerned about something.

"Yes. My brother is racing in it. He has a white Jeep." I begin to wonder if he is feeling okay. "Is something wrong? Are you lost?"

"No." He points. "It's that way."

"Yes, it's on the map. Do you have a map?"

He checked his back pocket. "My map! It's gone!"

His friend held up a map. "You dropped it when you were running."

"Thanks." Danny took it back.

I continue to wonder why he ran up to me. "Are you with a parent?"

"Yeah. They're up ahead. They went that way."

"Ok. Do you live on the Dreamboat?"

"Nah. We live on the ground. We live in Nature Trail Estates."

I have a hunch where he'll sit at the next race and why he wants to sit there. A serious look is on his face, and it makes me concerned. I try to lighten up the situation whatever it might be, so I smile and speak in a friendly tone, almost as if I'm teasing him. "Are you going to sit in the front row again?"

"Of course!" A smile begins to curl up, more on one side than the other. I can tell that his buddies like his friendship, but they look impatient and distracted by their toys. Danny still looks urgent to give me an important piece of information. His smile disappears when he begins to tell me something. "I just wanted to give you a heads up. At the next race, the mud is going to be real watery. They always do it that way. I just wanted to warn you."

"Oh, I see. Thanks for the heads up. Are you guys going on the cruise ship?"

"Yeah, man! Aren't you? They have tours today!"

"Of course. Okay, well, have a nice afternoon."

"You, too. Bye!" They race off, firetrucks flying in the air.

I hear a voice call out from up ahead. Turning my head, I see an older woman waving her arm. "Danny!" She motions for him to hurry up. "Stay together! Achoo! Oh, the ragweed!"

I want to ask Stella if kids bother her, but I know better. It would be bad manners to say such a thing. Saying something like that out loud would sound offensive. I don't want her to take it the wrong way. I don't want anything bad to happen. I don't want to get another friendly knuckle zap from one of her arm slugs.

Someone else is running, and I hear footsteps from behind. A young man runs past us, trying to beat the crowd. He turns around while running backwards quacking. "I'm going to beat you!"

I don't run much, but I suddenly feel like running. Stella looks content with walking. The first runner has a big lead with a smug look on his face. The second runner looks even more determined to catch up.

With one foot in front of the other, Stella and I finally arrive at the Galaxy Dreamboat. We are allowed to enter a limited area for guests, and we soon learn that we can tour another limited area for free or follow the next guided tour for five tokens. Stella and I agree that a tour guide would be much more interesting. The next tour is scheduled to begin in ten minutes. Stella decides that standing in line would be much too boring, so I suggest exploring for ten minutes, but we can't venture off too far.

A lady behind the counter scans my phone and takes five of my tokens. She gives me a wristband along with a small piece of information. "Welcome to the Tritonic Galaxy Dreamboat. A *falling star warning* was issued about forty-five minutes ago."

"Has anyone seen one in this area?"

"That's right, honey. That's what a falling star warning means. You might see one or two at this time of day." She glances up into the sky. "Nothing to worry about. Falling stars happen all the time. They've been falling for billions of years."

"Really?" I ask.

"Really. Your brown eyes match your shirt."

"They're not brown. They're hazel."

"Well, they match your shirt. Next!"

How does she know they've been falling for billions of years? Is she that old? Seriously, it's not like there was a video camera back then to record it. She has no idea that I am, to a large degree, self-taught regarding historical data. My family sits on the fence with issues such as the *Age of Earth*, which only causes me to dig deeper and find out for myself. A big part of me has been left to struggle with a certain amount of wanting to know the truth, and not blindly believing in something just because someone else does. I've never been a 'jump on the band wagon' type. Something deep down inside of me has always wanted to examine the facts, seek out the truth, and not just take someone's word for it.

At one point in my life, I researched the philosopher's stone and the elixir of life. Information and opposing views are out there, but it always amazes me to hear some people believe in something based on guesses. The whole idea of a resurrection obtained my undivided attention. How did the heartbeat of Jesus start beating again? How can our flesh materialize once we are decomposed? Some things are difficult to understand, but I learned just because something is mysterious now, it doesn't mean that it will be mysterious forever. Back home, I have a quote by Neil Armstrong hanging on my wall. "Mystery creates wonder and wonder is the basis of man's desire to understand."

There was a short moment after the worker said *next* when I could have voiced my opinion or asked her how she knows the age of the asteroids. But what is my opinion? How do I know if falling stars were happening billions of years ago? I really can't argue with it. Besides, I've never been the arguing type.

Stella says nothing about the warning. She takes the information as if it is a new way of life, as if someone had just told her to have a nice day.

Will I see a falling star this month, yet once again? It makes me remember seeing a falling star in early March before the strike ever hit Asia. It was the first one I had ever seen in my life. I was thrilled to see it moving across the night sky. Now I dread seeing them. I wonder if they are going to land. Some of them are big weapons landing in random places on Earth.

8

ROOF DILEMMA

Cindy's World

I am standing with a tour ticket still in my hand. Stella and I know we need to stay in the area for ten more minutes. *Oh, my gosh!* My eyes widen as I look up. I see an enormous yellow slide starting at an upper deck, winding all the way down to the entrance. "Look at that slide!"

A large, beautiful photo of a falling star is hanging on display. It catches my attention, yet I despise the beauty, knowing how much damage it can cause. Danny is gazing at the photo.

"Wow! That's so cool!" says Danny to his father.

"A falling star is actually not cool at all." Danny's father seems familiar with the true nature of the beast. In a mature, confident manner, he informs his son and his son's friends about falling stars. He looks at the sign next to the big photo and takes the time to explain.

"It says here that it can travel up to 30,000 miles per hour and have a temperature as high as 3,000 degrees Fahrenheit. A falling star can turn into a fireball or touch the ground. And if it does touch the ground, it is no longer a falling star. It is called a meteorite. And meteorites, my son, are what came down and attacked our neighborhood in May."

Danny's face quickly changes from admiration to mild fear as he gazes at the image, slightly tilts his head, and appreciates the photo from a new angle. His caprices have made his demeanor appear sharper, wiser, and more mature as he turns his head away from the image.

I place the ticket in my front pocket, appreciating the beauty as well as the danger of flying rocks.

A tour guide leads a small crowd of people over to a display. It looks as though they are in the middle of a tour.

Stella is not paying any attention to them. She is speaking to Danny's mother about all the free things she gives away at her parties. "This month we are giving away a free gift with a purchase..."

A red blinking light on the wall catches my eye. The wheels of my mind turn a new gear. I'm intrigued. Another light next to it is steady, and it's the same color of red. A third light is turned off. I look at the tour guide to see if he is concerned with the red lights, but he pays no attention to it. No one seems to be alarmed. The guide says something to his group, and I want to hear what he is saying.

"Let's go over there." I suggest to Stella, and she agrees after considering my idea. We head over to the tour guide.

He speaks loud so that everyone in the immediate area can hear. "...and at certain times of the year, the Earth passes through a comet trail. There can be as many as one hundred falling stars in one hour, or you might see as many as forty falling stars at the same time. Usually, rocks that are less than eighty feet in diameter will burn up before it can reach the surface of the ground. That's a good thing, right? It is estimated that millions of falling stars will be seen from this location over the next seven years. This is one reason why we built a one-of-a-kind Galaxy Dreamboat. We have sophisticated telescopes. We take a lot of pictures. We want people to appreciate the beauty in our universe. Of course, we also enforce safety. All of the glass on the Dreamboat is not your regular kind. For safety, our glass is shatterproof. We recommend that you stay away from glass, in general, when you get back home, if you can."

He continues in a listenable tone. "Speaking of windows, if you don't mind, you can no longer replace a window with another window. Windows that have been blown out should be replaced with wood, shatterproof glass, or a strong wall. A strong wall is much safer than a window when a meteorite hits."

A man cuts in with a question. "But how can we tell if a falling star is going to collide with the surface of Earth? Don't we have any technology to determine when a collision is going to happen?"

"Yes and no. Making a prediction of exactly when rocks will fall from the sky is sort of like determining if it is going to hail." The tour guide has a name badge that reads, Officer King. "In the past, on average, around five hundred meteorites touch down on Earth each year, but only about five are found, and the ones that we do find are usually the size of a baseball. But in this year alone, it is estimated that over ten-thousand meteorites have touched down, and many more falling stars have exploded like a fireball, causing shock waves and major destruction."

"Oh, that is so gnarly, dude." A young tan surfer man with bleach blond hair is the only person who is smiling.

An awkward moment permeates the crowd, and several heads turn to see who made the comment. Then the surfer realizes that no one thinks it is cool except for him. His smile diminishes as he raises his eyebrows and widens his eyes.

"Oh, you know, dude. I just meant like, you know, man. Like, wow, you know."

The tour guide walks us to a new area and directs our attention to a meteorite on display, the only big one in the lobby.

"This meteorite is called Mezeppa. Please use the hand sanitizer if you want to touch it. It was found in Mezeppa Park after the strike in May. It was discovered by soccer players. You can see that it is ten-feet wide, and I can assure you that it must have been much larger when it entered the atmosphere. Some meteorites that landed back in May have been found to be as large as a half-of-a-mile-wide, many of which are in the bottom of the ocean. Three of these super rocks have been found in the ocean, in more shallow water, down in Key West. These super rocks are also called *mega meteorites*. Unfortunately, some of these mega meteorites landed in cities, towns, and suburbs. Earth will continue to experience thousands and thousands of falling stars over the next seven years. We have entered into dangerous times, and we want to help prepare people for the next round of strikes."

The surfer is not happy with this news. He frowns and clears his voice. "Are you telling me it's going to get worse, man?"

"Most likely, yes. It's difficult to predict which meteors are approaching Earth because they travel at different angles and different speeds, sometimes colliding with each other in space. And it's even more difficult to predict where the meteorites will land on Earth because of the variation in size and speed. It appears that the worst of it might happen during the fourth year, when most of the meteors will drop at that time."

"Oh, dude, how bad is it going to get?"

"It's possible that it might be like this, year after year, for the next six years." The tour guide remains calm while the surfer moans.

"Oh, man!"

A woman speaks up with a curious look on her face. "Excuse me, why is that red light flashing?"

She points and people from the tour group look in the direction of where she is pointing. There are two large maps hung on the wall. One is a map of North Carolina. The other is a map of the world.

"The flashing red light on both maps means that a falling star has been located somewhere. It was flashing almost non-stop in March, April, and May. The steady red light on both maps means that a meteorite has touched down somewhere. We had no red lights at all in June and July. Now it's flashing again. The big light that is off will turn on if a mega meteorite has touched down anywhere on Earth. Many meteors, maybe hundreds, are approaching Earth right now, but they'll burn up before they can hit the ground. Good thing, right? If you turn to your right, you can see many smaller meteorites up close in the display case. Now that our tour has come to an end, please feel free to view the rocks on your own. Please use the hand sanitizer before you touch the big rock."

Another woman yelps loud enough for the tour guide to hear. "Excuse me? You have glass on the ship? I can't believe it. Glass is banned! All glass should be removed."

Stress from this new way of life clearly has her rattled in a state of panic.

"Remember what I said earlier. The Dreamboat has armor strong enough to withstand a meteorite strike. The display case does not have your typical glass. It's made of a special netting substance that won't explode into pieces." Calvin glances at his watch. "We're all out of time. I want to thank you for being a part of this tour group. Please pick up a brochure on the way out if you have not already done so. If you caught the last part of this tour, another one will be starting in about five minutes. And if you made a reservation to stay the night here, welcome, and I hope you enjoy your visit."

A few of the people immediately break away from the group while most of the other tourists linger on to view the sparkling super rock.

They seem confident, using shatterproof glass. Hmm. It must be safe on this cruise ship. I'm starting to feel safe, I tell myself.

I have seen too many glass buildings on the news to know that glass can turn into a deadly, spontaneous weapon. Whoever designed this cruise ship has gone to great lengths to make sure this place is safe even if the rest of the world is not. He made a strong effort to educate citizens on the dangers of glass.

All this makes me miss my lamp back in my bedroom. It's where I read all my favorite books.

I notice one woman who walks away, and I decide she is someone who doesn't want to be standing anywhere near glass when the next shock wave hits.

She grumbles as she almost brushes my shoulder. "There's no telling when a fireball is going to explode, and I'm not going to take my chances. I'm getting out of here."

I step away from her and step closer to the large meteorite. The surface of the iron meteorite looks like a normal type of a dull brown rock with sparkles, but I know that there is nothing dull or normal about this rock. The crust looks somewhat smooth like an apple. I can see metallic tinted flecks, and the sign says that it is made of an element called iron-nickel. It's hard for me to imagine that rocks like this one, as big as a half-of-a-mile-wide, have smashed into Earth and will continue to do so for the next six years, as they say, in the months of March, April, May, and August.

A woman about forty-years old turns to me with a disturbed look on her face. "Did you hear about the roof?"

"The roof? No. What about it?"

"You have to sign a waiver in order to go on...the roof."
The woman sounds frightened. "The main door to the roof
says, *Enter at Your Own Risk.* It's like being on top of the
Rockefeller building." She is speaking with fear in her voice.

"No, it's not, Rosey. Stop that," her husband interjects,
trying to calm her down. He thumps his foot on the ground.
"There isn't any glass up on the upper deck, and the
Dreamboat is not as tall as the Rockefeller. The Dreamboat
is wide open up there. And it's called the upper deck, not the
roof. They painted a line, and you have to stay behind the
line. So, stop calling it the roof. This is a cruise ship for
crying out loud."

Rosey ignores her husband's rambling comment and
thumping as he groans and turns away.

Rosey leans in toward me, so her husband cannot hear.
"I almost passed out. You could be taking your last breath
up there."

"What do you mean?"

"They say you can go up there to watch the shooting
stars." Her voice was little more than a murmur.

"Did you see any?"

"No. I'm not going to stay up there to see a shooting star. I went up to see the roof because my hubby made me go with him. I don't even like being outside because, you know…" Rosey points toward one side of her neck and moves her hand across to the other side. "It can happen at any moment. There's no way to know if the falling stars are going to burn up all the way or…." She makes a hand motion as if something has blown up, and her face begins to sour. "Poof. A fireball, or worse…" Her face puckers like she had just tasted a lemon. "It could be another strike. Here one minute," she whispers the last few words with a choked-up tone, "and gone the next just like my sister, Ruth Anne. God bless her."

"I'm so sorry," I say, feeling sad for her sister.

Rosey looks up toward heaven, shakes her head no, and then her eyes look down. She looks as innocent as a kitten meowing. "The world is changing. We can never step in the same river twice."

"What did you just say?" I ask.

Her husband heard everything. He leans in toward me. "Don't listen to her. She's just afraid of heights. Always has been."

I want to be polite, but a smile does not feel natural in this moment. "Well, thanks for letting me know about the tour up on the top of the—."

"Upper deck. You're welcome. Go check it out. Maybe you'll see a shooting star. We didn't see one, but maybe you will. Nothing to worry about. They say it looks different up there at night. They say that at night, the stars look more brilliant up there than they do from the ground. It's another world up there." The man breathes heavy and shuffles away with his nervous wife.

I notice Rosey turning back to look at me while her husband is not paying attention to her. Rosey makes sure that I can see her. A look of worry is on her face, and it almost makes me respond by mimicking with worry. Instead, I hope that she will not be plagued with fear for the next seven years.

She points up, shakes her head no, and whispers. "Don't go up there." Then she points down. "Stay here."

I wave a little good-bye, turn away, and let out a small huff. I don't want her to think I am laughing at her, but it is unreasonable to think that we can't go outside ever again.

The metallic flecks fascinate Stella. She examines them closely. "It looks like it has gold in it or somethin'."

"Well…I'm sure it isn't real gold." I say to Stella, not surprised at her wishful thinking.

With so much stress and anxiety floating around, no wonder the Dreamboat has a comedy show after dinner on the weekends. I feel like I need to de-stress after seeing that big rock. I point to a sign. "Look. It says they have a comedy show tonight. I wonder how much it costs."

9

ENTER AT YOUR OWN RISK

Cindy's World

I am curious as we walk through a secret passageway.

Calvin is greeting the guests in a cordial and enthusiastic manner. "This way to the upper deck!"

"I'm amazed at all this stuff you' tellin' us about. I hope to see one of them shootin' stars, you know. Do you think we'll see any?" Stella asks.

"I can't promise anything, but I'll try to make it happen," Calvin answers.

Stella does not respond to his humor because she's looking at everything.

"Hi! What is your name?" Calvin asks me.

I find humor in his response and make a connection. "Cindy. Wow! Look at all those lifeboats!"

"Welcome to the upper deck! Please find a seat."

Once everyone is settled into position, Calvin begins to give us more information. "Certain ancient teachers of science have promised the improbability of meteors touching down in such large quantities on Earth. Well, they were wrong. As we all know, the May strike changed the world. You are going to find out here and now that three years ago, we identified asteroids approaching Earth with such a high probability of collision, that they began talking privately about designing a ship.

"Going even further back, about fifty years ago, we learned that it was very possible for Earth to experience a devastating asteroid strike. Recently, though, we have been able to determine that the heaviest strikes could possibly last for a total of seven consecutive years. The data, at first, was not conclusive. We couldn't prove that this would happen, and the government prohibited any mention of a possible wipe out unless it could be proven."

Calvin appears to be about twenty something years of age. He carries himself with a smile of great benevolence. A few lighter brown hairs are seen on the sides of his head, but those at the top and back are dark brown. His height is not short, and his voice is the voice of a charming salesman. He speaks in lecture style, although it feels much more casual as if he, too, was learning. He continues to explain the possibility of us seeing a falling star. "At this time of day, we might see a falling star in the northeast."

As Calvin goes on, I begin to grapple with this palpable enemy. Life must go on, yes, but it is a different world in which we live. So many changes have been made since May, and yet we continue to seek ways to locate the dread of all dreads, a half-mile wide asteroid approaching Earth. Calvin explains that improvements have been made to locate objects in motion near Earth, but newer, more advanced technology is still needed.

"We are working hard to achieve much more. Our current satellites have located a meteor storm for this area in North Carolina. A falling star warning has been issued and estimated to last until five o'clock tonight. The best time to see a meteor shower is at night during a clear sky. It's harder to see the falling stars during the—"

"Hey, look! Over there!" Danny points up toward the left.

"That, my friend, is a meteor," Calvin points out.

The group waits to see how far it goes. It happens to burn out rather quickly and seems to vanish.

"So, that one had a short fiery tail. At this time of year, Earth is going through an asteroid path. Meteor showers are more likely to be seen on Earth during the warmer months, and this is why we have seen several storms in March, April, May, and now again in August. Remember, a falling star is really not a star. It's a rock."

"WOW!" Danny points.

Suddenly, our group sees ten to twelve falling stars. They have long fiery tails, longer than the last one, and seem to be falling closer to Earth. One by one, they disintegrate.

"Those are very small meteors, maybe even as small as a grain of sand. When you see a light streak that is very thin, it means that they are very small."

The light show and hissing sound continue for another minute.

Finally, Calvin speaks. "I am happy to have witnessed this light show today, and if our enthusiasm equals, I have no doubt that you have enjoyed this time up on the top of the ship as much as I did."

He continues to explain that most of the groups on the top deck only see one or two falling stars. Some of the groups don't see any.

"Our time has come to an end on the upper deck. Let me conclude with this. Astronomy is the branch of scientific study in which much has been made known about the stars, planets, comets, and galaxies. At the same time, much is left to the department of human knowledge to further discover more and more about celestial objects. It's time that our group heads back downstairs, but I invite you to meet me in the lobby where we will finish the tour. There I will tell you about the mega rock. At this time, I need to ask you to head back to the grand staircase and—"

Suddenly, a single falling star, wider than any that had been seen, appears in the northeast leaving a long smoky trail. The tail is glowing brighter and brighter until at last, moving closer and closer to the ground, an explosion is heard. The sky looks like an unusual whiteout. The bright flash lasts for only a second, not much time for a response from anyone, while something sounds like a jet is flying by.

When visibility returns, Calvin prepares his group for what to expect next. He calls out in a loud voice. His calm nature is not shaken by all the murmurs floating about. His instructions are given with an air of frankness, aiming to banish any fear of the unknown.

"We will experience a shock wave at any moment. Everyone, remain calm. It's best to wait it out. Do not run. Do not go to the staircase. We will get through this sonic boom. It will pass by and soon be gone. There is no need to panic. We saw a brilliant fireball thirty times brighter than the sun. It escalated into full illumination. We call it a whiteout. Please remain in your seats," Calvin explains in an orderly way.

A dull whistling sound is heard as if something is flying. A few of the eyes are darting around to see how others are responding. The group has an overall look of uncertainty while waiting for something to happen.

Danny is amazed, looking around in the sky. "A whiteout! Dad! Dad!"

Narissa's husband rubs the back of his neck as if he has an ache.

The sound begins to fade. The effects look minimal and void of any damage at all.

Narissa frowns, scrunches her lips, and speaks with sarcasm. "Oh, look, it's an alien! Get me out of this place."

Calvin smiles, knowing that the cosmic show has, most likely, ended. He smiles big enough and long enough. One by one, several people take a deep breath after the wonder of this cosmic event has finished. Those on the upper deck are relieved that the aftershock is over.

"It might pass all the way around Earth. We might hear it again. The aftershock probably knocked down some trees and blew out some car windows. It's a good thing we are out in the middle of nowhere. Our instruments will be able to tell us how fast the shock wave was traveling."

Another dull humming sound is heard, but it's much different than the previous one. Calvin's attention is fixed on the sound with great suspicion while respecting the delicacy of human feelings. He presses record on his camera. He speaks slowly while looking into the distance. "Wait. Something's not quite right."

He pauses, analyzing the sound, and then considers the possibility of a second passing.

"Mr. King?" I step forward with great concern.

"I don't know. This sound is something different." He continues to listen, and then he looks up.

"Mr. King? What is it?"

He focuses on the sky. An unusual darkness is seen straight up over head. It is dim at first, but then it becomes darker, breaking wide around the ship. Calvin steps to the railing, looks down, and I can hear him mumble into a mouthpiece. "Better days ahead."

The group is directing their attention straight up.

Narissa becomes dizzy and speaks in a serious tone. "Hey, I'm feeling light-headed. What's happening? Is this a UFO?"

"My legs, man!" The surfer yells out. "They're heavy! What's going on?"

I trudge after Calvin and slow down. "Mr. King! What is this?"

"Not sure." Calvin looks up again.

"What is that cloud?"

Stella manages to drag her feet one last step, walking up behind me.

From the tour group, Catfish yells out. "Bon voyage!"

Any stage of discovery is clouded by a sensation of being unable to move.

"My feet, man!" The surfer yells out again. "I can't pick them up. Is this, like, the end of the world?"

"It betta' not be," Stella says. "I have three kitchen parties."

"Is that a UFO?" I ask. "Oh, my legs! What is this?"

The tour group becomes immoveable. Calvin manages to speak a few more words. "I have a hunch, but I don't think you're going to believe me."

"At this point, we might believe anything," I say. "What do you see?"

"It looks like a shadow is covering the ship."

"A shadow? From a UFO? Do they want to take us up? I admit, lately I've been wanting more in my life. But now it looks like this might be the end. This might somehow be my fault. I should have been happier in this world."

Calvin looks shocked and fatigued. "I can guarantee, little lady, that whatever is happening, this is not your fault. Is your name Jonah?"

"No."

"Good. We won't make you walk the plank."

"It's Cindy."

What had been the study and desire from the wisest space men is now within the grasp of something unknown. Like some type of magic scene, the tour group along with the Dreamboat and all the contents on the ship begin to fade underneath a shadow. Almost like a passage to another life, the ship is beginning to travel.

"I can't move!" I cry out.

"It's really happening!" Calvin yells.

"What is this?" I yell.

"Oh, boy! Let's hope we arrive in one piece."

"One piece? Where are we going?"

"This is it. We're traveling. Here one minute...gone the next. We're on our way to a hiding place. We can only hope for a safe return."

A power so magnetic, a power so abundantly overwhelming, is freezing the body of each person, but without any change in temperature. Every intricacy of fiber, muscle, and vein is locked into complete stillness until speech is no longer possible. A great work of science and mechanics is baffling everyone on board, seeming to take everyone by surprise.

"Do we need life jackets?" Stella asks.

"It's too late," Calvin says.

I thought this was possible, but I never thought it would happen like this.

"Law Four!" Catfish calls out. "Trust Jesus as your Lord and Savior!"

The deck begins to fade, and the voices come to an end.
I can feel my heart pounding and then one more pound.

10

ARRIVAL

Cindy's World

I am standing somewhere with unremitting ardor, but my body feels weak, emaciated beyond description. I cling to the hope of arriving, landing to exist once again. I am experiencing a mixture of surrender and curiosity, and my body feels heavy. A wave of sinking sensation flows through me. I cannot conceive the variety of feelings that run in my mind, from enthusiasm to suppressing panic. There is no longer any ability to fight against something beyond my control. My life flashes before me until all I can see is darkness. At last, I lean not to my own understanding, but I trust my life in the hands of our Creator. Finally, I sense a wave of surrendering peace and see a speck of light, knowing that I am blessed with His grace. I can feel my body traveling, to a new time or the same time, I do not know. I am still thinking, and, in the process, I try to feel my toes.

I consider the type of destination as complex and wonderful as heaven. I feel broken and embarrassed for wanting so much more from my life. The more I try to find my life, the more I feel as though I am lost. Lately, my life feels like I've been hunting in tall thick grass. I think about some man's last words before I was taken. He had guessed that we're on our way to a hiding place. I can't argue about the incredible nature of his hunch, although the possibility of a UFO is still hanging high over my head. One way or another, we are moving in space. I spend a good amount of time thinking about my body parts, and hope as the man does, wanting all the pieces to arrive in good condition. I think about another man's words and repeat them. "Trust Jesus."

Off in the distance, I hear a loud horn blast long, low, and steady. Slowly as if coming out of a dream, I begin to hear the voices of people one at a time, and I wonder whom they might be.

"This is gnarly, dude!" A male voice sounds familiar. He sounds basically content with his arrival.

Another man's voice pleads, sounding desperate. "Aahh! Narissa! Speak to me! Narissa, honey! Say something!"

Out of the blue, it dawns on me that my life hasn't belonged to me all along. The situation at present hardly leaves me to understand anything else other than my lack of ability to do much of anything. My imperfect body and voice are at rest, and my mind continues to surface with the hope of a successful destination until I return.

Next, I hear two men exchanging ideas. I hear one man's voice speaking to another. They sound familiar.

"Boss! What happened?" Catfish asks his supervisor.

"Hmph! Maybe a UFO took us, you dip-nard."

"Abducted by aliens? No way, we're in the ocean. I bet we'll be on the evening news."

"Hey, Catfish, what's up with my cell phone? It's dead. What o'clock is it?"

"What are you blabbering about?"

"My cell phone. It's dead. You got the time?"

"I dunno. Captain said we'd lose some time. He said it might happen. He warned us." Catfish speaks in a pleased tone.

"Yeah, but did you ever think we really would?"

"I don't know, boss. I guess so. Didn't you? You okay? Drake? Hey, Drake!"

"Stop it. I know my name, you chunk of rotted seaweed. Now we're never going to make it to the next mud race."

"Why not?"

"Catfish, we're in the ocean, you dunderhead. Let's go find Sam." Drake says.

I doubt at first whether I should attempt to travel into the unknown as a person of great adventure, or one of the simplest forms of existence. It is highly unlikely that we traveled at the speed of light, but my imagination has expanded way too much in just a short period of time, and it seems unreasonable to rule out the impossible.

A moment of uncertainty is felt when my surroundings begin to look like I am still on the top of the same ship. Far off, it looks different. In the distance, I see a horizon where the sky meets the sea. I dedicate myself to figuring out my identity, yet my name I cannot recall. I first notice the afternoon sun and then a man comes into focus. His face and uniform begin to look familiar. The time of day is unknown. With an unreleased breathlessness sense of anticipation, I conclude I had just traveled to a location that someone had called the hiding place.

My limbs tremble as I exhale, and my eyes swim in remembrance. *What has happened? Where am I? What is my name?* For a moment, I cannot recall any person in my life except for a woman from New York. I see her face and I can hear her voice from recent memories. She looks vaguely familiar, which makes me search hard for any recollection of what I had been doing last. Forcing myself to recall her first name, I grasp for a new strength in my voice. It comes out as a whisper. "Stella?"

I have returned to my body although just previously, I had lost all sensation. Slowly, I make a fist and understand tremendous secrets to the human frame. The woman I know as Stella blinks but says nothing. I see a familiar man more clearly, and his name floods my mind when I hear his voice.

"Stay behind the red lines!" Calvin shouts in a mellow tone. He reaches into his pocket and pulls out his cell phone.

I am engaged, heart and soul, urged by an eagerness to see where we are at. *Where am I?*

A woman moans, sounding like she is in pain. "This isn't heaven."

There isn't any moaning or crying in heaven. No, we are not in heaven.

A frantic impulse slightly bends my knee when I think of my parents calling my name. Then suddenly, as if the last few pieces of a puzzle had just been fit into place, I know who I am and this tour group becomes my new reality, which leads me to urgently find out where we have ended up.

At the top of the ship, and separated from the cabins and staircase below, the air on the upper deck feels different. It smells like gunpowder mixed with a fresh, warm salty breeze. Overhead, a flock of seagulls cry while they glide about in opposing directions. It makes me aware of a new sense of tranquility and a taste for simple pleasures in which nothing can mix in to destroy it. I am engrossed in a quiet moment of still composure, and a vision of my old life is but a leaf falling to the ground. My body relaxes and I can turn my head. Much to my surprise, my shorts feel baggier. I take greater notice of my inner peace when I hear a ship's bell ring two times. I feel my muscles supporting my body and take another deep breath. Each bell sound lasts for about ten seconds, and it seems to be coming from somewhere, silencing the entire group.

Calvin raises his arms above his head to get our attention. He speaks with a sense of determination in his voice. "Our ship is at sea. For your own safety, stay behind the red lines!" He looks at his cell phone while tapping on the screen.

A lone white seagull glides, landing close by on the edge of an empty railing. He has black tipped wings. He is a clue that we must be close to land. The air grows thick with moisture as mist swells into existence.

"Mr. King, where are we?" I ask.

"The coordinates say twenty-five degrees North, seventy-seven degrees West."

"Where's that?"

He lifts his head. "Somewhere north of Nassau. We're in the Bahamas. Captain Sam has issued a town hall meeting."

"What time is it?"

He glances at his cell phone. "It's 4:00 p.m. Eastern Time Zone. Our group is to report to a town hall meeting right away."

I glance to the right. Another woman looks familiar. *It's the woman who had been sitting next to Stella at lunch.*

She is swaying to the left as she tries to take a step. Her knees buckle. Then she stumbles and lands in a chair. Her eyelids are tightly closed, and her body looks like a lifeless form. She opens her eyes and squints. She carries a heavy look of anxiety on her face that amounts to agony. Her head tilts down again.

"Narissa? Are you okay, babe? Narissa? Say something." Her husband rushes to help.

She looks in his direction. "We're doomed, aren't we?"

"No. No, we're not doomed. We're on our way to a town hall meeting. Can you get up?"

"I saw Jesus! I was with Jesus! Oh, I'm so tired. My legs feel flimsy. I don't know what's wrong. My legs feel like I can't walk."

"Make sure you tell your therapist all about this when we get back home. Our group is leaving. We have to go. We have to go downstairs. We can't stay up here any longer. You need to walk."

I grow alarmed at Narissa's weakness. It could be me sitting in that chair and unable to walk. *What's wrong with Narissa?*

"I can't. Can you carry me?" She appears to be thinner than what I remember. Her husband picks her up, and she wraps one arm around the back of his neck. He carries her to the door where a crewman is directing people to meet Captain Sam down at the First Mate Theater.

"Cinderella!" I hear someone call out. Stella's eyes are wider than her mouth. She walks closer. "What on Earth is goin' on?"

"I don't know. I think we'll find out at the town hall meeting. That's where we're going. Are you okay to walk downstairs?"

Tears fill her eyes. She chokes out a few words. "I think so. Wait. I can't remember my name. But I remember yours. It's Cinderella, right? What is happening?"

I look into her eyes, wanting to give her the little strength I have. Shunning my concerns, I die to any alarm of her lack of memory. Knowing full well that my name in Cindy, I cannot heap on any more confusion into her world. I reject any ounce of incipient fear that Stella's memory might not be intact.

From out of nowhere, I seize a new energy in the purpose of my life. In this moment, our friendship is all that matters. I've never seen her like this. She is much less confident. "Yes, that's right. My name is Cinderella. Your name is Stella and I am your friend. The important thing is that we're still here...somewhere. Looks like some people aren't doing well. We're on a ship, and we're on our way to meet the captain at a town hall meeting."

I knew what it was like to have lost my name. It is a blank feeling of vulnerability. How can I ever describe my emotions at a time like this when other people need to find an ounce of hope? Never did I ever have the desire to give this type of hope to anyone.

Different aspects in life are not so changeable as the development of human nature. My feet could very well remain my feet, but my doubt can brilliantly change into courage. This magnificent change contrasts with Stella's watery eyes. I want to give her some faith, but I know that it is not my gift to give. Her sole purpose in life had been to throw kitchen parties. I wonder how much she can remember. Nevertheless, I do not ask. She has no choice now but to accept the change of this bizarre circumstance, this mega catastrophe.

We had arrived, some not as fortunate as others. Narissa looked as though she had been deprived of rest and health while others walked away scot-free. A few people hurried on with disgust written on their face, and yet others drifted away looking refreshed and energized, as if they had just got off a roller coaster. Previously, I had heard the rumor of a quantum leap, but I did not really believe it would happen to me. Perhaps a part of me had challenged the occasion. I can't accept the possibility that aliens had just abducted us. Unable to compose my questioning mind, my inquisitive nature is alive and well. Even if this isn't a quantum leap, my mind is set on finding out. More than ever before in my life, I sense a need to put the pieces together.

Stella and I rush toward the door. Our legs are functioning perfectly well. A considerable amount of newness is felt in my human body, and it makes me want to buy a new belt. I feel embarrassed over the fact that I had worked so hard at searching for a better life when I should have been searching for the truth about who it is that has given me life. From the looks of it, not everyone has experienced this newness and it disturbs me.

I approach the open door and see a Dreamboat man in uniform. The dim light of a yellowish lightbulb shines down on the man's face. His dark blue eyes are fixed on me. His white short-sleeve shirt scarcely covers the work of muscles beneath. Why didn't I notice this man before? His yellowish skin and his dark hair set him apart from any other.

He smiles. "The town hall meeting is on the first floor in the First Mate Theater. Take the yellow slide all the way down."

I test my memory. His nametag reads *Officer King* and I become aware of my recollection. "You're our tour guide."

"And I live here." He seems to be testing his own memory.

"You look familiar."

"So do you." He smiles showing his shiny white teeth.

"What kind of officer are you?"

"I'm a Security Officer on deck."

"Weren't you our tour guide?"

"Yes. That is my job. I do both."

"I have a lot of questions."

"We all do. Go to the town hall meeting. Do you have a reservation?"

"No."

"The passengers who have a reservation will stay in their room to get a news report."

Stella nudges me from behind.

With ten thousand people below, the journey to the theater could have been dismal, not knowing how many people have arrived in one piece. I can't imagine a cruise ship theater being able to hold so many passengers. I follow a trail of curious people down the slide and methinks it is pleasant that my legs are working mighty fine. The change is irreversible. There is no walking out to see Piper at the mud race. Our location has been identified on Calvin's GPS. Once Stella and I slide down to the first floor, I notice a clock tower indicating four o'clock. A crewmember motions with his left hand, and he points in the direction of the meeting.

My phone buzzes.

It's Piper. "We just had a big earthquake! It was an 8 magnitude! Are you okay? What happened?"

11

TOWN HALL MEETING

Captain Sam's World

He has too much work to do. Captain Sam walks past his brown leather chair. Out of habit, he checks his silvery water-resistant compass watch which records time to the nano-second. The satellite clock on the wall in his study reads 3:58 p.m., yet his watch reads 1:40 p.m. He changes the time on his watch. "One...two...and..."

Then he finds his custom-made telescope.

He is gray at the temples and lives to be at sea, a true bon vivant dedicating his life to traveling the world while, strangely enough, skimping by on small bars of cheap brown soap. Carefully, he slides his telescope into a hidden porthole, which is safely tucked away in his study. He levers the scope all the way to the right and looks in. His eyes bulge wide as his dream has come true. "We're back, Leah!"

He looks through the scope. The sky is holding back the rain. A blurry horizon reveals a formation of mist on the waters.

"Twilight is in three and a half hours. Daylight's a burnin'," he mumbles.

He walks over to a microphone and speaks a command. "Sound the arrival call."

He moves to the automatic window panel and pushes a button in his study until the western sky appears. "I need to see more!"

He smooths his gray scruffy beard with his left hand, impelled to hurry along the window opener. He mumbles impatiently. "Find me a high-speed window."

A solid panel slides open, conveniently to the right, opening his study to the west. He peers out. He searches the sky in case an unwanted drone is lurking nearby.

He takes in the whole gamut, inhales the salty air, and lets out a big breath of relief. "No danger in sight for now."

The arrival horn interrupts his thought.

He inspects his legs, stretches his arms, and cracks his left elbow. "Ah, we made it."

His eyes dart to a high shelf where he looks for his hidden box. His stomach turns as a moment of fear opens his eyes wide, and he hurries to his door with irregular steps. "Still locked."

He returns and grabs his prized hidden box. Looking inside, he sees his pet and photos are still there. "I'll get you fixed up, my little pet. No one can ever find you." Sam pauses a moment. He examines the small parts, squinting his eyes, and mumbles to himself,

"Pass the word for Walter...Where are we?" He shuts the lid and places the box back on the shelf.

With accurate use of celestial navigation, the captain takes hold of a sextant. He measures the angle between the sun and the horizon. He investigates the eyepiece and determines a latitude location of 25 degrees north, and then he compares it with his modern GPS. It's the same.

He glances at a world map and walks back to the microphone and gives another command. "Helmsman, set course for Nassau!"

"Aye-aye, Captain."

He hears three beeps.

The voice of Officer Mina travels through a speaker. "Captain, Sir?"

He looks in the direction. "Yes? Pour it on."

"Looks like we made it, Sir. We shut down the entrance. No one can leave unless, of course, they jump or walk the plank."

"Very well."

"The town hall meeting begins in a few minutes. If you're feeling well, they're expecting you, Sir."

"Yes, I will be a few minutes late."

"Thank you, Sir. If there's anything else I can do for you, let me know."

"Send my three top officers to me at once."

"Yes, sir."

He hears two beeps, indicating the conversation is over.

Captain Sam paces in his luxurious study. To release the stress, he exhales and looks out the secret window.

A faint bell rings two times, each ten seconds long.

"Ahh, it's four o'clock. Walter, my friend, you snoop! Why are you spying on me?" He speaks with jovial disgust into the air.

Sam looks out the window and scans the ocean all the way to the horizon. He sees no sign of being followed.

After several paces, he walks to the bookshelf to glance at a picture of his wife, hidden in the pages of a book by Edgar Allen Poe.

"We dreamed of the day we'd be together, sailing the seas and seeing the world. Heaven took you too soon." His breathing slows down as he sees the photo. "Your eyes are bright and beautiful. Your voice is music to my soul."

He reads her handwriting on the back.

Sam, I know what love is because of you.

Love, Leah

Feeling a phantom lump in his throat, he fingers down the table of contents until he finds it, City in the Sea.

"Your favorite poem." His eyes fill with warm tears. He sighs and opens his eyes wide to keep them from falling.

Turning to the page, he reads the lyrics, speaking a few lines out loud:

But lo, a stir is in the air!

The wave - there is a movement there!

As if the towers had thrust aside,

In slightly sinking, the dull tide -

As if their tops had feebly given

A void within the filmy Heaven.

Holding onto the book for just another moment, he walks to a pendulum swing on his desk. He is keen to lift a silver ball. The click, click sound and transfer of energy amuses him. It also relaxes him.

He hugs the book, closer, and looks out to the sea. Nothing could equal his delight more than Leah. His memories with her hold dear in his recollection. Her very existence had been a part of his life year after year with no children of their own. He whispers, "I miss you, Leah. Your eyes, your touch, your voice."

After he closes the hidden window, he returns the book to the shelf—the book that had belonged to his beloved wife.

Captain Sam continues the ship's work at hand. As he proceeds out the door, three officers from Deck and Engineering stand in the hallway in front of his study.

"Any casualties?" the captain asks.

"Not that we know of. It's too early." Chief Mate Maurice speaks matter-of-factly, holding back any concern.

"Zero's a good number. Stay behind me and keep me updated as soon as you hear from Medical. We set course for Nassau." Sam can always count on Maurice.

"Yes, Sir."

The four men head to the town hall meeting.

"Captain Sam, you're looking well. How glad I am to see you." A passenger greets the captain with a handshake and leans in to speak more privately. "It looks like you made it all in one piece. There's a bald lady who claims she lost her hair during the transition. Not everyone arrived holus-bolus."

"That's what I hear. We will get to the bottom of this." The captain carries a look of delight and joy when he greets them under these alarming circumstances.

The First Mate Theater fills up and overflows with tourists. The captain addresses the crowd.

"You might easily accept that we are here due to something called a quantum leap, or this could be the most difficult thing in all the world to understand. I won't lie to you. The situation that we are in is not an easy one to explain. But don't worry. We have enough food and water to last a few days, and there's no reason to worry about going hungry."

Someone in the audience blurts out in a rabid manner. "Captain, how long will we be at sea?"

"Let me finish and then if you have any questions, you can ask. As I was saying, we have enough food and water to last for a few days out at sea, and we are close to land. We have already set course, and we are expected to reach the port at Nassau in three days. We plan to stay in Nassau for two nights, and then set course to Florida. My staff and cruise directors are prepared to provide you with an enjoyable experience. The staff is ready to help direct you to wherever you need to go. If you ever get lost, you should find directories and hospitality managers throughout the ship. Security Officers will be on patrol 24/7, some on bicycles, some on stand-up scooters."

The crowd whispers amongst themselves.

"Quiet, please. One free meal will be provided for three days from 5:00 p.m. to 8:00 p.m. starting today in all the restaurants. We have seven main restaurants that can each hold about five hundred people. Passengers have been divided into three different times for dinner. Your group here has been assigned to the Seahorse Cafe for a dinner anytime from 5:00 to 6:00. In order for us to get dinner served to all the passengers, we ask that you show up at the proper time or up to thirty minutes early or up to thirty minutes late. The people in this group have been given a first-class stateroom in a wing that is currently unoccupied. This wing has not gone through inspection, but everything should be in good working order. We will give you a keycard in the lobby when you exit the theater. We will hold another town hall meeting tomorrow at four o'clock. That's pretty much it for now. I can take a few questions, and then I need to get back to work. Please raise your hand. Yes?"

"Captain, some people are not doing very well. My wife is unable to walk. I'll be honest with you. I'm really upset at whatever did this to her. She was fine one minute, and then we see a big flash in the sky, and the next thing we know, we're stuck here out in the middle of an ocean and there's something wrong with her legs." The man holds his wife around the waist as she leans on him.

"The emergency number on the ship is 211 for security, technician, and medical help. You can ask any crewmember for an ambulance cart, and it will take you to the Medical Department. We have nurses and physicians to help. We even have a chapel where you can go to find some peace. Remember, this is a big ship. The Galaxy Dreamboat is a city in the sea." The captain turns his head to an officer. "Can we get an ambulance down here right away?"

"Yes, Sir."

"Any other questions? Yes?"

"Captain. Are there any casualties?" The surfer asks.

"So far, none have been reported. Anyone else? Yes?"

"Captain, what in the world happened? I mean, where are we? And how could something like this happen? If we are here because of a quantum leap, then who is responsible for doing this to us?" A tall man pushes his glasses on his nose.

"Several good questions. I promise that after a more thorough investigation, a detailed explanation will be given, and we will find those who are involved and hold them responsible. At this time, all I can say is that a quantum leap is the best way to explain how we ended up in the Atlantic Ocean. As far as where we're at, our coordinates show that we are just north of Nassau, which is southeast of Florida. Any other questions? Yes?"

"Sir, how long will it be until we can get back home?" Sam hears another voice in the crowd.

"It'll take three days to get to Nassau. We'll need to stop at the port to get some supplies, which could take up to two more days. When we arrive at Nassau, you can leave and make your own arrangements, or you can stay on board while we set course to Florida."

"Captain, my cell phone doesn't work!" A voice shouts from the back of the crowd.

"Well, if you didn't sign up for a world-wide cellular plan, your phone is not going to work. We have a telecommunications department in case you want to make a phone call. Any other questions? Yes?"

"Captain, my watch shows that we lost about two hours and fifteen minutes. Is that how long we went missing?"

"We are in the process of forwarding the clocks, and yes, the clocks seem to be behind about two hours and fifteen minutes."

"Captain, as ridiculous as it might sound, some people are saying we were abducted by aliens. Do you think this true?"

"No. Any other questions?"

"Captain, are you saying that right now, there is someone out there who did this to us? A person?"

"That is a good possibility. We're not sure. We have a team of investigators on this ship, working around the clock, to find out who is responsible. Once we find out who is behind this, law enforcement will carry out justice. If you find anything unusual at all, please report it right away to security, and we will look into it. It's important to stay calm during this crisis. Thank you for attending the town hall meeting. We will hold another town hall meeting tomorrow at four o'clock. No more questions for now."

Captain Sam pushes his way through the crowd. He reaches one of the space agency employees.

"Top of the day to you, Captain. How's the wind?" A look of approval surfaces on one of the space agency faces. He is the principal investigator, Walter Mandelbaum, and he shakes the captain's hand.

"Better days ahead. Let's talk—privately in my study—right away."

"At your service, Sam. I've been waiting for you to spill it. After you."

Most of the guests are leaving, but a few linger in the theater to discuss the critical matters further.

12

PRISON ISLAND

Cindy's World

"Yes, I'm fine. Are you okay?" I ask.

"Yes. What happened?" Piper asks.

"I don't know. We're in the ocean. They said we went through a quantum leap. Tell mom and dad I'm fine. In three days, we'll get to Nassau, and then we can fly home. I have to go. Stella and I need your help booking us a flight."

Stella is unusually quiet. She sits in the First Mate Theater after the town hall meeting, looking down. She accepts what happened but tries to find a way to bounce back. Making eye contact with me, her face is pale. "Tell me again how we got here."

"Okay, well, we were up on the top of the ship, as you know. We were watching the falling stars. Do you remember that part?"

Her eyes look down for a moment. "Not really."

I have never seen Stella act this way. She's childlike. How do I get her to the Medical Department?

"Everything was fine at first." I couch down to her level.

"Then what happened?"

"Then we saw this huge flashing light. It was a fireball, I guess. There was a humming sound and Mr. King told us it was a shockwave."

Stella stares at me with no facial expressions. "A shockwave?"

"Your face is sort of looking pale. Are you okay?"

"I want to know what happened after the big flash." Stella shifted in her seat.

"Okay, well, I don't know what happened to everyone else, but my body felt heavy, like I couldn't move. I was stuck like a statue, frozen, I guess."

"And you were standing up?"

"Yeah, but my legs couldn't move. I could still hear and talk for a little bit. I heard Mr. King say we were headed to the ocean."

"He knew where we were going?" Stella's eyes widened.

"Come to think of it, yes. He did. Some people were saying that the Dreamboat might evaporate, but I didn't really believe it."

"Evaporate? Hot water evaporates, right? I remember that."

"Yes. Yes, it does." I feel a sense of joy because some of her memory had surfaced. "You know, I'd feel a little bit better if I found a nurse to check you out. Just to be safe. Are you feeling sick?"

"No. I'm just tired. I can hardly remember anything."

"I bet the nurse knows what to do about it. Let me take you to see a nurse. It can't hurt if we see a nurse, right? I'll find someone to help."

"I want to walk." Stella opposes even though she is fond of golf carts.

"You know, you have a lot of kitchen parties when we get back home."

"Oh, yeah! You still need to buy some spices!"

We chuckle as a security cart pulls up right beside us.

"Hey, there. You ladies doin' okay?" A man asks. He shows us his work badge on a lanyard. His first name is in big bold letters, OLIVER.

Before Stella can say anything, I respond first with a serious, urgent tone in my voice. "We're on our way to find a nurse."

"I took another woman to Medical. Her feet were paralyzed." Oliver rests his right arm up on the back of the seat next to him.

I can hardly believe he relays this shocking bit of personal information in a casual manner. I sense a need to bring balance to the conversation before Stella completely loses it.

"It could have been worse. As far as I know, no one has lost any arms and legs." I try to look on the bright side.

"Not true. A guy was rushed into surgery."

"He lost his…" I begin.

"His arms *and* his legs," James says.

"Oh, no." For a moment, I look down in shock. My effort to bring balance is lacking. *Try something else.* "And how are you doing?"

"I'm fine." His left hand lets go of the steering wheel.

"Is the Medical Department busy?"

"Not really. Last time I saw, there were about six or seven people down there. They'll get you right in. Did you see the big flash?"

His cart has plenty of room for Stella and me.

Is he ever going to ask us if we need a ride? "I saw it when I was up on the upper deck."

"Wow! How was that?" His eyes widen in interest.

"It was a whiteout." I answer.

"I was down in the lobby, and it lit up. I guess we'll be asking everyone where they were when the big flash hit."

I say nothing of his bottomless remark, disapproving of his flagrant, chatty nature during a critical moment.

He points. "Did you know there's a show tonight? Look."

I see a poster that says, *Anchor Watch starring Cooper Grenado and Marlin Spike at 8pm.*

"We need a nurse," I say.

"Get in. Free of charge. I'll take you to Medical."

I help Stella into the front seat, and then I slide into the back.

"Hold on." He speeds away down the hall and casually notices that Stella is looking weak. He turns his head to the right and asks her a question. "How are your feet?"

Stella looks down a short way and doesn't know what to say.

"I said how are your feet. Can you hear me? Can you feel your feet?"

She becomes annoyed by his questions. She snaps back, "They're fine! Yes, I can hear you. And yes, I can feel my feet."

"Ho-ho-ho! All righty then, little miss two feet!"

I lean in so he can hear my urgent words. "She needs to relax."

We arrive at Medical without speaking another word. I am a tad bit worried, and surely nothing but a determination of avoiding despair could be more important. My friend needs to be restored to life, and perhaps she only needs a good rest. The human body, after all, has a way of recovering if it is given the chance to do so under proper conditions. My words have silenced the driver, but at least he is now paying attention to Stella's struggle, and he is not as interested in me. I keep watching for any ounce of worry to creep onto the driver's face, but he remains steadfast. Maybe it's best that he seems disconnected to the traumatic event. Maybe it's time I do the same, not that I want to grow cold.

At least we are headed in the right direction. The driver's inner strength becomes divine inspiration for me. I had mistaken him for being aloof, but he is fully aware of his surroundings. He truly does care. He wants to help us in his own sort of way. I'm aware of some new changes. My virtual leaves have already fallen. Somewhere deep down inside, I perceive young buds are shooting forth from a secret tree planted in the window of my heart. I made it through a near death experience where Jesus gave me amazing grace. Now I know what it is like to want others to have this new life. I am aware of new things that I had not seen before.

I can sense it. A new season is springing up in my life, which I contribute to this unpredictable journey. I feel a new sense of purpose, although I do not know exactly, but new sentiments of joy are present in a short period of time since the arrival. Usually, I dread going to the doctor's office, but a new purpose rises within me. I am more cheerful than ever and work hard to control this passion to help others survive. My phone buzzes. It's Piper again.

"Hi, so what's going on?" He speaks matter of fact.

"I can't talk right now. I'm fine. I said I'll call you later."

13

PRIVY INFORMATION

Captain Sam's World

The captain throws his door open, as children are accustomed to do when they want to get away from some bothering situation. He steps into his empty study, waiting for Walter the investigator. When he sees Walter in his doorway, he has another chance to get this right.

"Captain, I need to ask you a few questions." Walter shows his face in a serious, determined manner, looking directly at the captain and leaning slightly forward.

"Come aboard and bless my guts. Shut the door, you snoop. Not that it matters much where we speak. Any fly on the wall could be a drone, and so I'll remind you to keep your lips shut tight in public."

"I understand." Walter shuts the door. "As the old saying goes, loose lips sink ships. The drone revolution is here to stay. The only safe thing to say these days, almost, is that you have a drone." Walter used to be a lieutenant in the U.S. Navy Reserve, but he merged over to the U.S. Space Force. His phenomenal record of success landed him a job as a private investigator for the U.S.S.F. As a top-secret government agent, he is skilled in hand-to-hand combat and performs exceptionally well in times of a crisis.

"Someone says they own a drone, and that's all it takes. A person wises up. Expensive little suckers, aren't they?"

"Not really, Captain. I got mine for a hundred tokens. They're not as expensive as paying a helicopter pilot six hundred tokens an hour to go find your guy. So where's your pet or did you send it out?"

"I use mine for personal reasons."

"Come on, Sam."

"I do."

"You spy on your own friends?" Walter's upper lip raises into a smile, revealing crooked teeth.

"Quiet, you lousy snoop, or I'll chain you to the keel. When you're the captain, everyone is your friend, even your enemies."

"No more talking in circles. I'm going to find the person responsible for this if it takes the rest of my life. Did you want to talk to me about something, Captain? Because this matter is by far greater than ever before." The tone in Walter's voice sounds like he is growing thin on patience.

"It's going to come out in the news sooner or later." Sam looks to the shelf to make sure his box is still in hiding.

"Not unless you have one of these." Walter holds out an electronic device smaller than a cell phone.

"What is it?"

"It's a Rat Bird."

"Bless your old rusty heart. It looks nothing like a rat or a bird."

"It can play huckle-buckle and take out any drone. And according to my Rat, it says your drone is right here in this room. I found your spy, Captain. And I can take it out."

"Does your Rat penetrate through walls?"

"No. This kind operates on infrared detectors in open space. It can huckle-buckle, and I found your drone, Captain, in three seconds flat. It's time you spill it out."

"Bugger. I already found your drone spying on me."

"That's right. What comes around, goes around." Walter glances at Sam's hidden box on the shelf, smiles, and then sits down in one of the leather chairs. "You haven't been talking much. So you can relax now. It's just you and me and our drones and this Rat, and the media is a world away."

"I need to keep my job." Sam looks down in a moment of consternation.

Walter observes his friend's moment of mixed emotions.

"From one friend to another, spill it or I'll make *you* walk the plank." Walter speaks with command, takes the upper hand, and waits for a reply.

"When the space force offered me the possibility of a job two years ago, I didn't want it at first." The captain opens his secret window and then sits down in his favorite brown leather chair. "I sent my drone to spy on one of the guys to find out why the agency wanted to build a ship in the mudflats of North Carolina."

"Whom did you send the drone home to spy on?"

"Cain. I found out the agency didn't want to alarm anyone, but they detected a pending plate-shift near the Appalachian Mountains. When I learned the mountain range might very well collapse and sink into the Mississippi River and possibly send the entire eastern part of the United States into the Atlantic Ocean, I started to consider the job opportunity."

"And?" Walter adjusts comfortably in the other brown leather chair.

"And I took the job."

"And you kept spying on Cain."

"Aye."

"And?"

"And I found out Cain was fired for crossing over the line in the quantum leap department. He wanted to perform tests that were way too risky."

"So?" Walter asks.

"So, I watched Cain and his son-of-a-seahorse partner. They privately tested on small objects at first. Later on, I found out about the quantum leap satellite where they hover over objects and try to send them somewhere else. One day, they tested a motorcycle. After that worked, they tested a firetruck. After that worked, they wanted to test something real big, so they hovered over the USS North Carolina when it was empty one night, and then—."

"Did it work with 100% success?"

"No. One time it went bad, really bad." Sam looks out the window.

"What happened?"

"They found a human volunteer. Cain promised this guy, Owen, a free ride. They promised Owen a retired life in the Caribbean sipping on Pina Coladas after becoming famous as the first man to teleport. But something went wrong."

"Where did he end up? Do you have the location?" Walter's eyes open wide.

"Aye, but Cain went missing. Cain's seahorse went to find Owen. And the report he gave was not good."

"What was it?"

"A village woman was treating Owen for something she had never seen before."

"We're going to need the location of that village, Captain. Tell me about the village woman." Walter's voice is deep and slow.

"I saw an old woman inspect Owen's body. She said she'd never seen anything like it. She used medical terms, and it sounded like she must have been to med school. Owen told her she'd get in trouble if she mentioned it to anyone." He paused for a moment. "I don't want to lose my job."

"I see. Do you have the location of Cain?"

"No. He can operate the satellite from anywhere. His philosophy is quite simple. Each man to his own."

"You tell us the location of the village, and I'll make sure you keep your job as long as you cooperate with us from now on." Walter waits for another reply.

"Sounds fair. I'll make sure you never walk the plank." Sam remains in control.

"You can keep your dragonfly." Walter stands up. "I'm impressed. It deserves a medal of honor. You found all that from an insect drone. I'll throw in a real bird if you're looking for a real pet."

"No thanks, but I'll take a Rat." Sam pushes out of the chair.

"I'll see what I can do about that." Walter puts his Rat back in his pocket.

"How very kind of you, and how very good you are to keep me as the captain. Arrgh, you're a snoopier snoop than I thought. This whole time, I have wanted to tell you, instead of keeping it to myself. I've paced back and forth, imagining how we could speak in private. I feel the greatest remorse for those who did not arrive as well as we did. I am disappointed in myself for not saying something sooner."

"Don't go on about this, Captain. What's done is done. It's not like you're the one who's been moving things around. Cain will be on our radar soon enough, and since you look like a load has been lifted off your back, would it be too much if I ask you to keep this information private? We're not ready for a press conference."

"Aye. I will not mention it. I'll be glad to forget this whole mess and throw it overboard."

"Captain, you're a wise man and a prudent commander. You went this far, and I'm sure you'll want to know what happens. I'll send you notes to keep you in the loop, but first things first. You bring me the location of where the human volunteer went, and I'll bring you a Rat."

"Aye. How about five o'clock at the Seahorse Cafe?"

"Works for me."

"I'll tell you plain. I'll write the location on a piece of paper and give it to you at the cafe."

"Until our next merry meeting." Walter hands Sam a bonus check. "This meeting has proved to advance the case.

We are finally getting somewhere. We need to get to that village as soon as possible."

"I'll be waiting for my new Rat." Sam takes the check as Walter leaves.

Captain Sam shuts the door, locks it, and retrieves his secret box.

"Hello, my little pet." Sam looks at the pieces one by one. "If you weren't broken for the last two weeks, I might have known this catastrophe was about to take place. Arrgh, but no worries. Soon we'll have a Rat."

14

COMPLEX SYSTEMS

Cindy's World

I thank the driver for his help, and he gives me a small nod. He drives away, leaving me with a renewed sense of strength. I've learned to endure uncertain times. I misunderstood him for not being able to pay attention to a crisis. In all reality, his demeanor stands firm like a lighthouse. He is like a strong tower where those in trouble could take refuge.

Take it lightly because it could be a whole lot worse.

When I check Stella in at the Medical Department, the nurse asks me about my own symptoms. I tell her I do not have any, but the nurse says it is highly unlikely. The nurse presses the issue further.

"Any tingling in the feet?"

"No."

"Memory loss?"

"No."

"Is your skin the same?"

"My skin?" I look at my arms, and they seem the same at first.

"What is it? Can you tell if your skin is the same?"

"Well, my shorts are baggy."

"Ok. Let's get your weight. Take a seat and we will call you in."

Stella sits by herself and smiles as she looks around. The furniture and wallpaper are dull. The grayish silver theme is intended to be modern and clean, yet the contrariwise results are plain and boring. I notice one cheerful picture on the wall. It is a big painting of a simple, happy outdoor setting with grayish purple mountains, blue skies, several trees, and a pond underneath a yellowish beam of sunshine shining down.

I have mixed feelings about protecting Stella or letting her go. I can't do anything else for her. She has to see a nurse.

Does she even remember Vinny? I don't even want to ask.

Surprisingly enough, the exam is quick, and it goes well. They ask us a few simple questions, prick our fingers, and say they will run some tests. I ask as much as I can and soon learn Stella is far worse off than I thought. I avoid thinking about if I have to leave Stella in this place.

"We have an Assisted Living wing where we can take care of her 'round the clock. It's nice and big and there's a lot of fresh air. All the windows have safety screens like these."

"When can I visit?" The news hits me like a ton of bricks. My knees weaken, but I remain strong for Stella.

Is Stella that sick?

Nurse Monica gives me some information about the temporary living arrangement.

I keep myself from frowning.

I disconnect from any rising grief, and I speak using calm language. "Stella, listen to me. I'm your friend. They have a place where they can take care of you. They're going to help you eat and get dressed. You don't need to worry about anything, okay?"

Stella looks down, without anything to say. Lost in her own thoughts, she crosses one arm while her thumb and pointer reach to her chin.

"I don't know what else to do. They're going to help you get through this."

Betsy the Caretaker enters the room and introduces herself to Stella. She leads us to where Stella will be cared for day and night. Betsy says she'll be with ten other people in the same condition.

We arrive at the Assisted Living wing and right away, I know this is where she needs to be for now, at least until she gets better. "You're going to stay here for the night. I'll be back to visit you tomorrow, okay?"

"Ok." Her eyes light up as an innocent child. "Cinderella?"

"Yes?"

"Tell me about the big flash again before you go." Stella takes hold of a soft teddy bear from the bed.

I don't want to disappoint her. She seems to like it when I tell her about the whiteout. This time, I want to be sure to make it sound as pleasant as possible. "Well, we were watching the falling stars and then we saw a big falling star. It flashed really bright, and it lit up the whole sky. I've never seen anything like it before."

"And the sound?"

"There was a humming sound that lasted for, I don't know, maybe a minute."

"What did it sound like?"

"Sort of like a jet."

"I like jets." She hugged the stuffed bear.

"Me, too. Maybe they have some books you can look at while you're here. Maybe they have some with jets. We'll take an airplane to get back home, okay?" I turn to Betsy. "Do you have any books here?"

Betsy is as cheerful as benevolent approbation on a lazy Sunday afternoon. "We sure do. I can take her to the library as soon as she clears."

"Great."

Stella whispers to the bear, then looks at me. "It's ok. Go on. I'll be fine. Bye, Cinderella."

I give Stella a hug, reluctant to let her go. "Bye, Stella."

Accepting Stella's condition gives me great pain at this time. If it weren't for the supportive sensitive nature of Betsy, I'd consider taking care of Stella myself.

Betsy discusses the matter further with me in private. "Stella has a strong heart and will pull through with colorful results."

Her kindness almost quiets my thoughts, but my curious nature overrides it. Her smile leads me to seize contentment with a new sense of order. I want Stella to get well as much as she does. I am intrigued by the way her joy has risen to the same level as mine. I can trust her. Betsy's face appears to carry itself on a long journey across a bed of roses whether the sun is shining down, or the storms of life are crashing through. The fire of love for one another shines bright in the garden of her heart, almost as if she had been expecting this rare occasion. Nothing seems to shake her dreamy world as if she were a fairy godmother.

"I want you to hear this true word. Believe me, she is going to be alright. We have something that will probably help improve her memory over the next forty-eight hours. I have been sent here for such a time as this."

I exhale and my body relaxes. I feel relief Stella will probably be getting better soon, yet the whole process of the staff taking in passengers so easily makes me suspicious. I don't want to come across as ungrateful for the superior service, but I need to find out more. "Some people might say one thing or another, but the staff seems very well prepared."

"We are. The captain went to great lengths to make sure we know how to give proper treatment. He is taking this traumatic event very seriously."

"He knew these conditions would happen?" Goosebumps appear on my forearms as a chill runs down my spine.

Besty's voice is soothing. "Not exactly, dear. The big flash took everyone by surprise. It doesn't matter how the transplant happened. We can't go back and change the past."

"If you don't mind me asking, what exactly did the captain prepare you for?"

"For the patients and for the arrival. Not everyone believed it would happen, but the staff is ready to help anyone who needs assistance. Once the first few patients came in, we started to see a pattern. Problems with the feet, legs, memory, skin changes, weight loss, and a few have lost their hair."

"Almost sounds like chemotherapy, doesn't it?" I ask.

"It could have been a whole lot worse. Our DNA is a complex system unlike anything we've ever studied. Did you know that the DNA of a human has many similarities to the DNA of a squash?"

"I've heard that before," I say.

Betsy lifts her eyebrows. "I'm glad I didn't turn into a pumpkin. Maybe someday we'll learn how to change a pumpkin into a carriage, but for now, I'm living here, finding a way to treat people like your friend. She is going to be ok. She is making progress already."

"Thanks for everything you're doing to help." I feel an unwillingness to leave Stella in a strange place, before she has become acquainted with any of the inhabitants. In just a short amount of time, however, Betsy instilled in me a new depth for expressing steadfast hope in the moment, despite the circumstance. I chase away any selfish pursuit of living in uncertainty, which once had crept in and narrowed my life.

Betsy's gentleness has warmed my senses as much as a serene summer sky reminds me, I'm passing through this life no matter where I go. Her soft voice comforts my soul as if it were a luxuriant field blooming and filling me with delight.

"Oh, you're most welcome. Visiting hours are from three to four tomorrow. Don't worry. She's going to be fine.

Go get yourself something to eat. Remember, we're survivors, and so is your friend."

A new journey begins. I am fixed on searching for the right restaurant and later checking into my cabin. I accede with pleasure to tend to my health by quenching my thirst and getting my fill of nutritious food, possibly even seafood, but more importantly, I am consumed with determination to find out what happened when the dim light hovered over the ship. As I approach the cafe, I hear the ship's bell ring two times again from somewhere in the distance. I see a clock that reads five o'clock.

A host greets me at the door. In a deep mature voice, he expresses appreciation to another passenger and then turns to me. He is tall, tan, and has brown hair and green eyes. "Welcome to the Seahorse Cafe."

In the waiting area, I see a large flat panel screen with a picture of modern jukebox. The digital words read, Now Playing: *Yellow Submarine* by The Beatles. I see the lyrics run across the bottom of the screen. My phone buzzes again.

"I'm fine," I say. "Stop worrying."

Shades of turquoise dominate the carpet and walls, making a bold statement of underwater amusement. The rustic walnut woodworking is indeed divine on the chairs, the lower walls, and on the beams of the high ceiling. For a brief moment, I see a pattern of seahorses and symmetrical coral flowing throughout the carpet.

I am undisturbed by my thoughts which, during the town hall meeting, have pressed me toward helping in any way I can to find the person responsible for leaving so many people in a less than normal condition. I move through a crowd and a hostess greets me at a podium. She smiles, holds a thin black marker in her hand, and speaks to me in a delicate voice. "How many?"

"One."

"Would you like to sit at the long counter?"

"Ok."

"You can go ahead and seat yourself."

There are several occupied seats at the counter, save for three vacant on the end. I find my way and sit, pleased with the polished surroundings and delicious aroma of fresh cooked food. A waitress with the nametag, Colleen, stops by to ask me if I'd like anything to drink. She's in her thirties, wears a lot of make-up, and has brown curly hair pulled back. She's either fueled by coffee or the fact that the world might be coming to an end, most likely the previous, but possibly both. She is focused, working hard as if her life depended on it. "What do you want to drink?"

"I'll have sweet tea." I say.

"Ok. I'll be right back."

I notice a familiar face, the tour guide who showed us the way to the giant yellow slide.

"Lemon?" She asks me.

"Ok."

The tour guide reaches to move the chair back. Previously, he had said he is a security officer, and he was also the tour guide. My memory serves me well.

"You got it, honey."

Then I hear the tour guide speak to me. "Anyone sitting here?"

"No."

The waitress decides to get two birds with one stone, as if I am in a party of two. I imagine her to be one of those waitresses who can carry ten plates at one time while humming her favorite tune. "What can I get you to drink?"

The tour guide sits in a chair on my left. "I'll have the same, sweet tea with lemon."

Throwing off my endeavor to crack open the menu, I read his nametag, *Officer King.*

The waitress answers him. "You got it, honey."

I text my brother again. "I'm fine. Stop worrying. I'm flying home in three days."

15

CRICKET THE SEAHORSE

Captain Sam returns to his desk to write a letter.

Dear Walter,

I will be waiting, rather impatiently I assume, for you at the cafe to give you the location of the village. I am tempted to write only the address of where you should take your investigation, but first I must explain myself further as to why I didn't give the location to you any earlier. What would I do with my guilt if you arrive at the location and, instead of finding clues about Owen the human volunteer, you find no clues at all? How could I ever waste your time on someone who went missing? I wish to prepare you for more terrible news during this investigation.

Poor Owen is dead! He was a rather lovable human volunteer whose smiles had lightened the room and warmed the coldest of hearts. He had set his focus on living a carefree life on a sunny beach, and in doing so, he walked right into Cain's experiment, a reckless experiment indeed. Cain is guilty of much more than involuntary manslaughter, and as any investigator knows, we will need the proper evidence to get him the death penalty for a criminal act of illegal teleportation.

Let me describe how I know Owen to be dead. I have been journaling the events with my drone.

Back in March after the first strike hit, I happened to test my new dragonfly drone on Cain because he had recently been fired. I soon learned Cain scheduled to meet with two other men. When Cain and his partner met with Owen, I discovered Owen privately stepped forward as a human volunteer, and one of his rewards was a retirement location on the beach where Owen was supposed to live happily ever after.

During the meeting, Cain confirmed that his partner would be waiting for Owen at the arrival. Cain wrote down the address of the beach house on a piece of paper and gave it to both his partner and to Owen. Cain gave 5,000 to Owen as a deposit, and he promised another 500,000 once the transport took place. Furthermore, I learned that Owen's confidence increased because earlier, he witnessed several animals crossing over. Not knowing the extent of the dangers involved, I followed Cain's partner when I flew my dragonfly to the arrival location and waited, as any investigator would do.

Here's where it gets worse. Owen was supposed to experience a successful teleport as the 'first man ever' on a Tuesday when no one was looking, but he didn't make it through like Cain told him he would. It was terrible. I saw and heard the whole thing via my dragonfly, and there was nothing I could do. The damage was done. Here's what happened.

Cain's partner was in the arrival location waiting for Owen to come through, and my drone was hiding. I listened to a conversation Cain had with his partner, Cricket. They argued for quite a while on the phone. Cricket had seen the arrival when Owen came through. Cricket went on to tell Cain how Owen arrived with no memory, no hair, and other changes in his skull and legs. Cricket panicked and said it was a freak accident, and Owen should be put down like a bad dog. It was a moment I wish I could forget. I heard the whole thing from my computer. Cricket went on and on about how and where they should take Owen's life. While Cricket was on the phone with Cain, Owen snuck off and ran away by himself. That's when I began to use my dragonfly to follow Owen and Cricket as much as I could keep up with both. Cricket continued his search for Owen over forty-eight hours. Cricket sleeps from 4 a. m. to 1 p. m. It would take a long time to describe what Owen went through during the two days he survived. For the sake of time, I will tell you later.

Cricket finally found Owen's body, stretched out on the grass discolored and motionless unlike anything I've ever seen. He took it to a village woman who confirmed the worst of it that Owen's whole DNA had changed from a human to something else. Cricket was very earnest to bury the body and convince the woman to never tell anyone. There was no way to bring Owen back. He was gone. He had once been so bright and full of life! His sufferings are, at least, at an end. He knows no pain, and I plead with you that he will not be a subject in some laboratory.

I am eager to give you the location coordinates of the burial, according to my GPS, as well as some blurry photos. This might be enough evidence to put Cricket away, but not enough to catch Cain. I lost track of Cain, so I kept following Cricket to find Cain. My drone stayed at the beach house, spying on Cricket for several days. I considered maybe Cain did not want to work with Cricket any longer, but I was wrong. Just over a week ago, I heard another conversation and learned more shocking news. Cain reported with great accuracy when the next strike would hit and where. He determined that a powerful energy force behind the next meteor strike would be enough to transport something bigger. He's been using natural energy to carry out his teleportations. I learned Cain is operating an illegal satellite from his computer. Once again, Cricket would be at the arrival location while Cain set the coordinates of the next object. Then my dragonfly broke on the island. I had to sneak in at sunrise and get it while Cricket was sleeping. For the sake of confidentiality, let us refer to Cricket as the Seahorse. Let us refer to Cain as the Blackbird.

For these reasons, I am including four coordinates: the beach house where the Seahorse is living, the burial site of Owen, the arrival location, and the village woman who inspected Owen. I will hold onto the photos until you are ready to receive them. As far as I know, the Seahorse is still at the beach house, and a pity it is. He's living alone and still works with the Blackbird.

With very best wishes,
Captain Sam Bellamy

The captain proofreads his letter and folds it two times. He places it in an envelope and writes *Walter* on the front. On another sheet of paper, he writes four coordinates and slides it in the envelope. He seals it shut and unlocks his study door.

During his walk to the Seahorse Cafe, he is deep in his own thoughts. *If we bring Owen in, his name will be famous, but not for the reason he wanted to be famous. Arrgh, he walked right into a yardarm. What will they do with Owen in the morgue? As I do think, he stepped in a game of whip and pickle, and he lost. I like it not. I watched him dance the hornpipe and couldn't save him.*

"Good evening, Captain!" A passenger says as he walks past with his wife.

"By all that is great and good, we live to see another day. Good fortune with you and yours. My duty to you, ma'am." Sam musters to find an exhortation, slightly nodding his head down for a pleasant exchange and a rather hasty exit.

The couple walks on.

He sighs, casually brings the envelope close to his chest, catches a moment of privacy, and scans behind himself. *Blackbird, you barnacle-covered Judas! You're the half-man! My hands are itching to scratch the eyeballs out of your sockets for what you've done.*

Then Sam calms his thoughts. *Owen's a man for Walter now. To own the truth and hide it is without a doubt, a lonely walk to the gallows. Walter will soon get my affidavy, and then…soon, Owen will rest in peace.*

At first, Sam wishes to hurry on, for he needs to deliver the coordinates as soon as possible. A new thought slackens his pace. *Well now, farewell to Owen, but what of my Leah? To my sorrow, she had a terrible slip. Speak it all in a word, there was nothing I could do. Which is worse, saying good-bye or hanging on? I am saying good-bye to Owen. Must I say good-bye to Leah?*

He greets another passenger as he sets course to the cafe and eventually, he picks up his pace. Along the way, his phone beeps.

"Yes?" Sam answers in a more solemn tone than usual.

"Ho there, Captain?" Officer Maurice speaks in code. "Cock-a-doodle-doo."

"Yes, my good friend. Rooster, this is he."

"Here's an update on the casualties for you: Zero."

Captain pauses a moment.

"Captain, you there? You got your head on, sir?"

"Yes, yes, it is on. I heard your update: Zero. Bend your ear to this. That'll be all. I'll be wishing you a very good day."

"I bid you good-day, sir." Maurice hangs up.

Sam hangs up and mumbles. "Poor Owen. Bless his guts. Here's an update for Maurice: One."

Sam arrives at the café. He is given a warm welcome by the restaurant staff and a hostess seats him at his private table for two where he waits for Walter.

16

SEAHORSE CAFE

Cindy's World

I can hardly contain the multitude of questions that crowd my mind. The most disturbing puzzle is the way in which the transport took place. How disconnected every cell must have been during that time. One small alteration in the pattern of the DNA can bring about a significant change. Wandering, floating cells could have zipped me back together and formed me into a squash. I don't prefer to think about someone's life being taken away in such a horrible manner. My life. It could have been my life that ended. Although the process is incomprehensible, the transport could have left some people with a completely different body—and it did take the arms and legs from one person. I encounter the dread of a thousand nameless possibilities. I tremble.

Is it possible my body parts could have been switched with someone else's? If there are dogs and cats on this ship, is it possible I could now have some of the DNA of an animal? I shudder at the thought.

The Seahorse Cafe holds several hundred passengers who fill up on delicious food. The sun is going down in the west, and it's comforting to know some things have not changed. The laws of nature are still in effect with an everlasting beauty of calm and heavenly scenes.

A giant flat panel screen hangs on one of the walls, displaying the current condition of a grand and glorious sky. I continue eating my dinner, gazing on the serene expanse while the ship journeys on towards Nassau, and I continue to eat my Salmon Caesar. Over the course of dinner, the sky fills with dark clouds.

I am overcome with the need to reflect on the big flash. I hear people ask others where they were when the 'big flash' hit and where they were when they froze, and it draws my attention.

"Where were you when the big flash hit?" A waitress on my right asks the lady on my right.

"I was in my cabin. I never saw anything. Where were you?" The lady takes a drink of water.

"I was outside in the Verandah Cafe."

"What did you see?"

"It was a whiteout. People ran inside and took cover. That's when we froze. You know, we're survivors. The news is going to want to talk to us." The waitress steps away.

The results seem like a two-sided coin. It had brought devastating changes to thousands of passengers, yet it brought a heavy sense of gratitude for those who made it through.

"Did you see the big flash?" The waitress asks another customer nearby.

"No. I was swimming laps. When I got to the end of the lane, the lifeguard was blowing his whistle, and he told me to get out of the pool. I had enough time to sit in a chair by the pool. Then we froze on the pool deck. Did you see it?"

"Yep. The sky flashed white. At least you didn't freeze in the pool! You could have been famous. The first person to teleport in water." The waitress moved on to talk to other customers.

So quickly, the event has been incomplete because no one seems to be talking about the unusual dim light, at least not the passengers who were inside the ship. The sun is going down, and now is the time to ask questions while the circumstance is still fresh in everyone's mind. The tour group on the Upper Deck is destined to face a virtual storm of temporary fame.

"Mam, are you doing okay?" The waitress asks another customer, Narissa.

I see a gloomy look on Narissa's face. She speaks quietly, and I cannot hear.

The waitress gives a piece of paper to Narissa's husband and walks away.

I wipe my mouth, resolutely face the unknown, and continue, even though it seems like a huge beast to examine further.

"Mr. King, I keep thinking about what happened on the upper deck. The big flash came and went so quick, but the way in which passengers are speaking about the big flash is unsettling. My friend lost her memory, and I don't think it was from the whiteout."

"Please, call me Calvin." He takes a drink, and I bravely focus on the frightening event.

"When you walked over to the side of the ship, what did you notice? Do you remember anything?"

"I can't seem to think about anything else. My job in security requires me to protect the passengers and the ship. Something looked wrong when I saw a dark cloud of something above the ship. I keep seeing it over and over in my mind."

"The light change?" I ask.

"Yes. A darkness was above the ship. I noticed the light change above us right after the big flash. It was like a steady cloud of darkness."

"What do you remember?" I lean in closer, speaking in a private, quiet manner.

"It seemed to narrow in on the ship. It was like we were under a reverse spotlight, and it was closing in on the shape of the ship. At first, I thought my eyes were adjusting to the big flash, and they were. But once I gained a clear focus, I noticed we were under a dark cloud."

"It must have been a machine up in the sky. Do you think? Someone else must have noticed it."

166

"As of right now, it is unidentified, and could very well be classified as a UFO. Right now, no one really knows about it except for the people who were on the upper deck. People become mesmerized by the word UFO. Whatever it was, if you ask me, I think it must have been a satellite." He takes another drink of his sweet tea.

"Did you speak to an investigator about it?"

"Not yet. Have you?"

"No. I'm still trying to make sense out of what happened. Maybe it would be worth it to find out what the other people saw on the upper deck."

Calvin takes the last bite of his meal and swallows. "I'd like to call a meeting with the people from the tour group. Do you think you could help me find some of them after dinner?"

"Absolutely!" I say.

"If anyone could do it, the tour group could give witness to whatever was happening in the sky after the big flash. Sooner or later, we will need to report what we saw," Calvin says.

A big part of me wants to know what the rest of the people on the upper desk observed. "We saw something going on up there."

"Yes, but maybe someone else saw something that we didn't. I want to ask our tour group if anyone had a chance to look up and see anything. I bet if we put our heads together, we might discover more about what happened."

It's easy for me to conclude that Calvin's desire for getting the tour group back together could prove to be a useful move. It could even help find the person responsible for inflicting a crisis of this magnitude.

After the big flash, the heavens were clouded with something, and like Calvin, I want to find out more. Right when I am about to tell Calvin I will help him get some people together from the upper deck, Colleen our waitress returns. In a typical manner, I think she is going to hand me my check. Instead, she hands Calvin a piece of paper and looks at him with pity.

"The captain is sitting over in his booth, and he wants you to join him. If I were you, I'd follow orders, or you might have to—you know, walk the plank. You were on the upper deck when the big flash hit, weren't you?"

"Yes, I was."

"Word's getting around you were on the upper deck." Colleen is speaking rather loud.

Another waitress hears her words, and she responds casually while continuing to move by. "The sharks are close by. I can feel it. You know what I mean. Which is worse, a human dart board or a private meeting with the captain?" She chuckles, looking away.

Calvin ponders her words with a poker face.

"Good luck, and may the sea be ever so friendly." She places Calvin's check face down on the table, and then she does the same to mine.

What could be so bad about reporting what we saw? The way in which Colleen said *good luck* makes me think she's glad she doesn't have to speak clandestinely to the captain, and she feels sorry Calvin is forced into a spontaneous, private meeting. Captain Sam can't be that bad, can he? He's seems friendly enough with the guests, in public, at least. I suddenly consider more possibilities. Is there any potential that the captain is part of this whole terrible event? Was it an accident? Who is responsible?

I see the captain is sitting with another man. Most likely, they are out looking for suspects. Knowing I have a history for being misunderstood, I'm glad Calvin has been called to the captain's table, and not me. I suddenly feel sorry for

Calvin, but I am confident he will do well when speaking to the captain.

Colleen piles on her concern with another statement. "They say a private meeting with the captain can lead to trouble unless you have a good attorney."

Calvin is direct. "Who is he sitting with?"

"Must be an investigator. That's my guess, anyway. Good luck."

She widens her eyes and lifts her eyebrows. "May the sea be ever in your favor."

Then she walks away.

"I hope your meeting with the captain goes well. I'll wait here. I'd like to know what he says, so I'll order dessert and wait."

Calvin takes his check and surprises me with a suggestion, as he is about to stand up. "Come with me."

"What?" I ask.

"Come with me to the captain's table."

I've never been one who is very good at making up an excuse. In this moment when I need to find my way out of a situation, my mind goes blank. I look down for a moment, searching for a way out.

Stay here. Whatever you do, do not go over there.

"If the tables were turned, I'd go with you," Calvin says.

He made a good point. But I am not him. I remain in my seat. I sit heavy and still.

After the way Colleen had looked at Calvin like he has just received a terrible misfortune, I think it's best if Calvin takes this meeting alone.

"What if they have a recorder?" I ask.

"A recorder? The whole booth probably has bugs and drones all over the place. So what? What better way for the story to come out? Whatever we say, it has to be the clear and solid truth."

"Calvin, I'm not a reporter or an investigator." I feel my palms getting sweaty and I wipe them on my shorts in a nonchalant manner, pressing down and lifting my shoulders. I rest my hands again and adjust my shoulders.

"You're an American citizen, and you were on the upper deck when the big flash hit. A lot of people are going to want to talk to you. There isn't a better place to start telling our story than at the captain's table."

"I don't have much of a story."

"Yes, you do. They'll want to know what you saw. Details can make a difference."

"Look, I don't know. You're invited to the meeting. Not me."

"Yes, you are. I just invited you. Maybe you'll learn something new." He stands up.

I exhale, look down, and back up at him. "Ok."

As I say this word of agreement, I'm dreading any slight chance of a conversation in which one small slip of the tongue could bring about the walking of the plank. *Where is the plank anyway? I hope I never find out.*

"When you speak, Cindy, you'll be speaking into an invisible microphone."

"You mean you have a drone?"

"Of course. Don't you?"

"No. I never thought I'd ever need one."

"My job in security requires it."

Calvin's phone rings, and he takes a quick call. "Um-hum. I see. Ok."

He hangs up.

17

UNEXPECTED SUSPECT

Captain Sam's World

The snoopy investigator sits at the captain's table. He finishes reading the letter, takes a drink of ice water, and licks his lips. Looking up, he questions the main suspect.

"How can this be? I worked with the guy for years. He was always a good pal. Even when he was fired, he still had a good reputation. Who is ever going to believe that he is behind the teleportation?"

"I'll carve your gizzard and fry it for my dinner, Walter, if ye smart off again. Is a blowing gale of wind on your side of the table? Did you see the curse of the chirping seahorse and his sinister blackbird in my letter?" Captain Sam speaks the last few words with an overly succinct pronunciation.

"Aye, Captain."

"We need to find the blackbird. I followed him as long as I could. I saw what I saw. There's no telling me he's not the man. The only way to the blackbird is to close in on the seahorse."

"You made it clear in your letter. The evidence you have points to finding the seahorse first, but it's not enough to commit him and a guy with a good reputation. All you have is circumstantial evidence the human volunteer was buried." Walter explains further. "People are buried every day, Captain, but it doesn't mean they killed the corpse. Right now, all we have, at best, is a dead body, and even manslaughter is highly debatable. We need to get our hands on the body and send it to the morgue."

"We'll examine the coordinates back in my study. You're going to need a few more things." Captain Sam follows the protocol of not mentioning the names of any of the suspects.

"Like what?"

"Things to dig up a dead body, of course. Long-sleeve gloves, a breathing mask, a shovel, a body bag, and security."

174

"Aye, aye, Sir. Sounds like a case I can handle. I should leave as soon as possible with the aid of security. Tonight."

"Operation Dig…" Sam ponders.

The waitress returns, asking Sam and Walter, one at a time, what they would like to eat for dinner.

"Did you find the Dungenous Crab?" Sam asks.

"Not yet. Still looking for it. What else can I get you, Captain?"

"I'll have the Turtle Pork 'n Doughboy with a side of flamingo tongue." The captain takes a drink of ice water.

"I'll have the Salted Beef Stew with a side of biscuits."

The waitress memorizes the order, smiling with a small nod. "Coming right up."

The captain waits until the waitress is gone. "Make fast. Even if you're tempted to arrest the rotten seahorse, you also need the blackbird. I want 'em both."

"I know you do, Captain."

"Now listen to me. The blackbird cannot be underestimated. We make him our final target. His good reputation can be our advantage. Sooner or later, the blackbird is bound to surface. He's a very smart man. Bugger, if it were up to me, I'd feed both the blackbird and his rotten seahorse piece-of-trash chirping partner to the sharks."

"I know you would, Captain. You'd make him walk the plank. We're not allowed to use any such method of torture."

"Threats are the oldest trick in the book even for an old gizzard like me. For the record, I am not torturing anyone."

"I know, Captain. Neither am I."

Walter then reflects that, the day on which Cain was fired, an attorney had escorted him out to his car. It had been a quiet removal when Walter saw Cain leave the building. Cain had given his office key to Walter and left without making a scene. "We need to take into account the blackbird's motive. If the blackbird was bitter about being fired, he never showed it. At this point in time, it's best if we do not give out any names as suspects until the case is more fully developed. We want the blackbird to feel comfortable enough to show his face in public. If he continues to live underground, we'll hide out at the beach and spy on the seahorse for as long as it takes."

"I'll get one of my security officers to help. There's someone I want you to meet. He was on the upper deck when the big flash hit. I want to send him with you to the village. He'd throw his life in front of a bullet to save yours. He's a good man. I'd trust him with my life."

"Who is it?"

"Calvin. He's on his way over as we speak."

Calvin and Cindy stand at the side of the captain's table. Calvin smiles, arms resting at his sides. His demeanor portrays a favorable outcome. Cindy's arms are crossed, showing her auspicious approach.

"Captain, Sir, your note sounds urgent," Calvin says.

"Who's this?" Sam refers to the woman.

"Hi, I'm Cylinda."

"Who?" Sam asks. "Is that a new part on a motorcycle?"

"No, Sir, that would be a cylinder." Cindy uncrosses her arms. "I go by Cindy. I was on the upper deck when the big flash hit. Nice to meet you, Captain."

Sam reaches his hand out for a nice greeting. She shakes it with a firm grip.

"Welcome to the city in the sea," Sam says.

"Thank you. This is my first cruise," Cindy says.

"You picked a good time to visit." Sam speaks candidly. "This is the first dogwatch of the day. The second dogwatch is from six to eight. It's likely your name will end up in a history book someday. A list of people on the upper deck is being made as we speak."

"Hello, sir." Calvin greets Walter with a slight nod.

"Nice day for a chat," Walter says. "Now that we all know about the next dogwatch, let's get down to business."

"Captain, Sir," Calvin says, "I just received a call from Isolation. They brought in a passenger who was protecting a Hornet Drone. Security found someone with a highly specialized top-secret surveillance drone has been reported as stolen, and the detainee has made a confession. Hornet Drones are only used by the U.S. Military. The detainee is being held in Isolation and is being questioned. At the very least, the detainee could be guilty by association, but we're not ruling out involvement with illegal teleportation. The suspect will be handed over to the United States authorities as soon as we reach Nassau."

"The rotten piece of seahorse is locked up on my ship?" The captain slides a piece of paper and a pen across the table to Calvin. "The name of the detainee, please."

Calvin follows the strict protocol of keeping top-secret names out-of-sight and inaudible. He picks up the pen and writes the name. Cindy keeps her eyes on the letters as the ink makes contact on the paper.

The first name is uncommon. Calvin writes as Cindy has a clear view.

Calvin writes the last name.

Cindy leans in a bit. She is a bit more absorbed by the situation, attempting to make eye contact with Calvin. Her mouth opens slightly. Then she quickly regains composure and shuts it.

Calvin folds the paper in half and slides it to the captain. He reads the name silently, Stella Giovanni. Then the captain passes the piece of paper to Walter.

This strange piece of information sounds like a telltale from the planet of miscommunication. In an instant, unhappiness is impressed on the countenance of Cindy, Sam, and Walter. The only person who has welcomed the information with a fleck of jovial intonation is Calvin.

Disapproving the name, Walter responds with complete and utter travesty. "Nice work, young man. I will remind you that this is a private case. Any suspect in isolation will be treated fair and, until we learn more, the facts must be thoroughly examined, and the suspect name must not be given out."

"Put it in the tray, Walter." Captain Sam orders and Walter follows through.

Walter crumples the piece of paper and tosses it inside a circular tray located in the center of the table. The tray is made of polished mirror, a type of stainless steel. Captain Sam ignites a lighter, and the paper turns to ash.

Cindy's eyes protuberate. She avoids saying the name of the suspect. "There must be some mistake. I know her. She lost her memory. She is definitely innocent. I am sure of it."

"The detainee lost her memory?" Walter asks.

"Yes. I took her to Assisted Living." Cindy nods, affirming the innocence of her friend.

"She has already confessed," Calvin says.

"Confession with a memory loss is not credible. A memory loss will complicate things and slow down the interrogation. Cindy, how do you know her?" Walter asks with suspicion.

"Wait a minute," Captain Sam says. "Until we can confirm that this confession is legitimate, no one will speak the suspect's name at the captain's table."

Calvin cuts in before Cindy can say another word. "Captain, I am not assuming she is guilty, but security will take her confession seriously. It would be ludicrous not to. She says the drone belongs to her. It could very well be the link to finding the person responsible for the Dreamboat teleportation. I can't imagine any normal human being would risk the lives of over ten thousand people, and I assure you, I have no intension to announce the name of the suspect to anyone outside this booth."

"I'm pleased security is taking this lead seriously," Captain Sam says, "but you'd be wise to know that there is another suspect involved."

"Who?" Calvin pauses for an answer but continues. "Is the second suspect on the ship?"

"Not that we know of," Captain Sam says. "We have reason to believe there is a suspect who lives close by on an island. Walter is going to check it out, and I need you to go with him."

Walter responds to Cindy's consternation. "Sounds like you believe that the detainee is innocent. We will rely on a thorough investigation."

"I'm sure it's a simple misunderstanding…" Cindy says.

Walter interrupts. "No names."

"She's innocent. I'm sure of it." Cindy insists, speaking confidently under the aegis of her convictions.

Captain Sam motions for a waitress. "Meet Walter and me in my study at 6:15. We will review the plan."

"Yes, sir." Calvin shows his loyalty.

"Now if you'll excuse us, we'd like to eat dessert," Captain Sam says.

Calvin responds with an obedient string reverberating in his voice. "See you soon, Captain. See you soon, Walter."

The waitress returns to the captain's table. She is holding two identical desserts called Captain Cobbler.

"Captain, sir, your favorite, as usual." The waitress places Walter's dessert first and then Sam's.

"My favorite time of day," Sam says.

Walter and Sam have no problem finishing off the last bit of warm apple-blueberry crunch, drizzled with butter, vanilla ice cream, and whipped topping.

18

WEAPONS

Cindy's World

This is a terrible mistake for poor Stella, who took possession of a drone and claimed it as her own. *Why did she ever say it belongs to her? Stella!* I can't imagine what my friend must be going through. Everyone on the ship knows the people in the Assisted Living wing have lost their memory, hair, or function of their legs. Stella is accused of stealing a top-secret spy drone as well as being held as a suspect for the Dreamboat teleportation crime.

There is no way I can sit by and let her suffer through an accusation, as some pretended friends might unfortunately do. I must speak to Calvin at once, telling him what I know about her good character. I am well acquainted with her by way of Vinny and Piper's friendship. During the time we spent together, she appeared to be an amiable and benevolent human being. She had been living with her ill mother, tending to her needs and ensuring the elderly woman's comfort while also nurturing the depressed and malnourished citizens at kitchen parties. I cannot hesitate in conveying a simple misunderstanding should not be held against Stella.

"Calvin, I know her. Before the big flash, she was a kitchen party lady. She was really good at fixing meals and feeding people, but she can hardly operate a simple cell phone. The teleportation has taken her memory, and obviously she cannot think clearly. She's always had a liking for free stuff, and I'm sure she was tempted to keep the little drone when she found it, but it's not hers. You have to hear me when I tell you she's innocent." I feel like I am not explaining myself well enough.

"You mean the *detainee*. It's best if we don't say the name out loud." Calvin murmurs to keep his volume down. "If it

184

brings you any comfort at all, you ought to know I am reluctant in my suspicion. I've always believed in *innocent until proven guilty*. The problem your friend has right now is she claims the drone belongs to her. The U.S. Military takes theft, double agents, and treason very seriously. She'll be in Isolation for at least one night, maybe until we get to Nassau. I sincerely hope she will be declared innocent. Citizens of the United States do not have any patience when it comes to terrorists."

"Terrorist? I promise you, she...your detainee is not a terrorist."

"We cannot have any names leaking to the media. I'm not even talking about your friend anymore. There is another suspect on the list. He's on an island not too far from here. I'll be leaving tonight with Walter to go check it out."

Calvin's one-on-one speech calms me when I hear another suspect is in the mix. I am firmly convinced Stella is totally innocent of stealing a military drone. She has nothing to do with a criminal teleportation. Stella can talk to anyone about plastic containers and popsicle sticks, but when it comes to technology, forget it. She's better off mingling with the ladies, talking about lasagna, Black Russian Bundt Cake spiced with vodka and coffee liqueur. She's better at handing out party favors such as cupcake bubble baths and vanilla pomegranate shower gel than operating a spy mission. I have no doubt that over time, there won't be enough evidence to convict her. She has lost her memory, and in doing so, she cannot think clearly about what belongs to her and what does not.

When I last saw Stella, she smiled altruistically, assuring me she would be okay as long as she can visit with the patients, find a new cake book, and learn about jets. Endowing her loveliness to the new inhabitants, a childish beauty sprang forth unlike anything I've ever seen. She was welcomed with the greatest affection by the staff, almost a little bit too easily, as if they'd been waiting a long time for her to arrive.

Separating her from the company of people by placing her in Isolation is the blackest ingratitude for her insatiable display of being an aggressive extrovert. What an unhappy victim she must be right now in a room by herself.

Before the big flash, she spent her time finding hostesses who will open their home and invite friends to get together. She provides a warm presentation of how to nurture one another by sharing recipes, delivering meals, and offering hospitable company. After the big flash, I have not only lost a friend, but this world has also lost a good person who brightens the lives of many lonely people who get by on cheap rice. Stella possesses virtuous qualities, except for the compulsive desire for getting free stuff, which renders her a happy life. Did her desire of getting free stuff finally get the best of her? I guess a greedy notion of *finders keepers* placed Stella in Isolation. How can someone as innocent as my friend ever be convicted of such a complex crime, even if she does like free stuff? Now it is my job to further convince the investigator of her innocence.

There must be some way I can take care of Stella to avoid this attack against her. After all, I am the one who took her to the nurse for a visit. Then again, without me, she would have been lost on the ship. I am certain that, in her current state of condition, she has no ability to explain her innocence. With a justice system that relies heavily on who has the best story, I am greatly concerned about Stella. I believe she has no enemies on Earth, but as I search for anything that could help Stella, I ask myself, did the real criminal place this drone to set her up, knowing full well about her condition? One theory is that once Stella claimed the drone to be hers as a childish game of 'mine,' the false evidence had been planted. This has to be what happened and together, Calvin and I must convince Walter. Better yet, I'll tell them about this simple mix up *and* help them find the real criminal. I must do something to find the felonious person in order to save Stella and in doing so, it would save the rest of the world from a madman. I rush forth to prevent her record from condemnation.

"Calvin, what does it take to be a part of the security program?"

"Why do you ask?"

"Do you think the criminal is on board?" I ask.

"It's possible. Do you think the criminal is on board?"

"I'm thinking that the criminal might be on board, and he planted a stolen drone on my friend to draw attention away from himself."

"You know the criminal to be a male?" Calvin asks.

"That's not what I mean. I'm exploring possibilities. I want to help."

"Look. I've already thought about whether or not the criminal is on board. See, the criminal most likely sent a drone to the Dreamboat to spy around. Why would he put himself in danger by going through a risky teleportation? If anything, he hired someone to be on board. I don't want to alarm you. For the sake of your comrade, her identity must still remain unknown."

"I feel bad for my friend." I pause and search for an answer. "I want to go with you to the captain's study at 6:15. Let me help. Let me go with you. I want to go to the village with you and Walter."

"It's too dangerous."

"You invited me to the captain's table."

"That's completely different. When I go to the village with Walter, we will be investigating, and a large part of what we do is based on instinct and protocol. I don't know you well enough to know what you will do under pressure, and there's no time to train you on the Rules of Engagement."

"We have thirty minutes." My eyes never left his.

"It takes *weeks* to train. Training is where the preparation takes place." He looks away and shakes his head *no* in a small uncertain way.

"Tell me the basics. Tell me all you can and leave the rest to instincts."

Calvin humors himself. "Rule number one…we are forbidden to kill civilians, and at this point, our suspect is a civilian."

"I don't have a weapon, do you?" I lift my arms up and then down.

"Yes. Security is allowed to carry a gun on the ship. There is an arms room where the captain will take us to get more weapons if we need them."

"A weapon room…on the ship? Where is it?"

"Hidden. You can come with me to the captain's study to review the plan, but it's not up to me whether you can go on the mission with me and Walter."

"You sound like the captain is in charge of an army."

"To some degree, he is," Calvin says.

"It's up to the captain if I can go to the village?"

"No."

"It's up to Walter?"

"No."

"Then who?"

"The only person who can decide if you can be a part of this operation is you."

This is a strange piece of unexpected intelligence. Is there an army on this ship? Is the captain an army leader? It seems impossible.

I hasten to find more understanding. I absorb it's up to me whether to go with Calvin to the village. Then like an invisible wave of fresh air, I glance to the side, thinking about Stella's love for free stuff and how wrongly she is suffering for it. I think about the inhabitants from the Assisted Living wing and how wrongly they have become hapless victims by the unhallowed art of incomplete teleportation. In a decisive moment, with every ounce of human goodness, I decide to take action. I can't sit by and watch the world crumble. In this moment, my destiny is clear. I must do something to declare her innocence and help free the world from becoming one giant hostage in the hands of a person with reckless, destructive behavior, no matter how good his reputation might seem on the surface. My sole focus rests on finding the true criminal no matter where he might be hiding.

I give Calvin my final decision. "I'm in."

Nothing is more alive to my human mind than the rising anticipation of catching this cold-hearted criminal who played around with thousands of innocent lives. Stella is alone, but I am free. A sense of guilt flashes through my mind, moving me to make better use of my time. More alert than I've ever been before, I listen to Calvin when he tells me the basic Rules of Engagement. First, he covers self-defense.

"We have the right to defend ourselves against an attack or a threat of an attack. If the attacker is not armed, we use minimal force proportional to the threat. We treat all persons with dignity and respect. We always defend ourselves and our unit against gun fire," Calvin says from memory. Then he refers to a file on his phone. "These rules are from the Annapolis Handbook of Worldwide Rules of Engagement, also called A-Rowe. We are under strict orders to hold our fire unless certain circumstances reveal that we are under fire."

I am listening intently when I hear a bell ring two times in the distance.

"Why is that bell ringing?" I ask Calvin. "This is the third time I've heard it."

"It rings on the hour, every hour from four to eight in the evening. It's six o'clock."

Next, he finds another list on his phone and points out key aspects on targeting suspects. "We are required to protect civilians, suspects, and prisoners. Armed force is the last resort. Let's see, normally, if we are under a threat, we shout a verbal warning to the suspect, and we tell him or her to stop or surrender. I'm trained in Negotiating, so I'm allowed to use those skills. We capture drones without any warning. If civilians are in the area, we must get permission from a commander to use a weapon and follow all guidelines. We are required to visually identify and confirm the suspect immediately to the commander prior to engagement. If the suspect does not surrender or show any sign of cooperating and the threat is high, then we aim for the suspect's feet, hands, arms, or legs, never the torso or head. Warning shots are not allowed. If the suspect is not able to fight, we must hold our fire. Do you have a license to carry?"

"No."

"So you aren't allowed to take a gun. We will use force only if necessary. Are you getting all this?"

"I think so."

Then he moves on to authority. "I graduated from the US Naval Academy. We respect authority. Authority is given to those who are proven to use good judgment. We have no short cuts. We give no favors. A commander earns his position to give commands. The commander protects his unit, and we trust him. Everything you say and do will be examined for honorable judgment by the entire unit. If you break any rules or guidelines, you won't be invited back. No exceptions."

Then he scrolls to another section from the A-Rowe. "We have limitations on using drones as spies. We are not allowed to use any drone that shoots or inflicts harm on a suspect unless we have permission. You don't have one, but Walter and I do. We follow the commander's plan in detail. We listen and ask good questions.

"The use of satellites and drones for surveillance, communication, and navigation for citizen and military purposes, is *not* prohibited. However, it *is* prohibited to place any weapon of mass destruction, including nuclear and biological, in the Earth's atmosphere or in outer space including the Earth's moon, a satellite, or a drone."

"Calvin, you really think a teleportation satellite took us from North Carolina and sent us to the Caribbean?"

He shrugs. "It's starting to look that way. The captain will fill us in. He has a plan. He will be our commander. Walter is the highest-level investigator. In some ways, Walter can override the commander's plan, depending on the situation."

* * *

Outside the cafe, three men linger. Catfish, Drake, and Burdock the surfer take a break near the Seahorse Cafe. They are all wearing a maintenance uniform. One of them notices movement out of the corner of his eye.

"Come here, you little pet. I'll roast you for supper." Catfish reaches out.

"By the looks of it, dude, your supper is running away." Burdock speaks in a joking manner.

"Mercy's sake, Catfish, don't take it by the legs. Fetch it from behind—quick! Before it gets away," Drake says.

"Look at the claws! Dude!" Burdock calls out in amazement.

The three friends hear two long bells at six o'clock and make haste to what they have found.

"Bustle to it. Man up and grab it!" Drake orders.

Unbeknownst to how the critter got loose on the ship, Catfish lifts the Dungeness Crab from the back side. The hard-shell legs lever back and forth. "What should I do with it?"

"Throw it overboard, dude!"

"Heavens no!" Drake cries out.

"The claws are gnarly, dude! Keep it away from me." Burdock says.

"We're going to keep it," Drake smiles. "We'll sneak into the kitchen tonight and boil it for a midnight snack."

"Why are you always bossing us around like you're a captain? Where should I put it?" Catfish asks.

"In a bucket, man," Burdock suggests. "It needs seawater."

"Where are we going to get some of that?" Catfish is confused. He scratches his head.

"Let me see, the *ocean*, you dunderhead." Drake points out in a rather matter of fact way.

* * *

Calvin and Cindy pass through security on their way to a private wing. Before long, they are standing in front of a bulletproof door. It is closed with a sign that reads, Captain's Study.

Calvin rings the doorbell.

Captain Sam views a large map spread on a high table. It has an image of an island and the title, Rum Cay District. Standing in front of an open window, he locates the first destination, the burial site.

"Calvin's here. Get the door, Walter."

The captain gives another command in a microphone. "Anchor down, right away!"

Walter does not hesitate to open the captain's door. He lets both Calvin and Cindy into the room and shuts the door. "Come in. Ever been to the Jewel of the Sea?"

"Nope," Calvin says.

"Where would that be?" Cindy asks.

"Brace yourself. It's a lonely little island."

At a high table, Sam introduces the plan. "A human volunteer has died. Owen's death was directly caused by an illegal satellite teleportation. We have evidence that the sinister black bird and his crony, the chirping seahorse, are responsible. Here's the plan. We get in. We find Owen. We get out.

"Walter, we need to take the body to the morgue for inspection as soon as you bring it back. I'll have my helicopter move in and another team will get Cricket.

"Shipmates, bold adventurers and all..." Sam points to a location on the map. An expression of despair falls onto the captain's face. He pauses for a moment and shivers from a flashback. A fleck of revenge is heard in his voice that makes those who are listening tremble. "Here's where Owen was buried."

He speaks again in a calm tone. "Mark your GPS and take this map with you."

"Dead?" Calvin asks. "Wait a minute."

"Hear me, something unfortunate has happened to poor, dead Owen," Sam says. "We banish fear by remembering all those on Earth who will, sometime later, highly esteem you for finding all three, the blackbird and seahorse, but first, poor dead Owen. While we live, while we are willing to speak the truth to each other, here in this ocean of fair wind and beauty, we seek to reap the tranquil blessing of bringing the blackbird to justice. Let nothing disturb your peace, even when you walk into the jewel of the ocean and through the flames of hell, when you hunt for whatever remains of Owen's body. Bless my guts, it's an ugly dead creature by now. A love for life will prevail in the end, my friend."

As the captain speaks, instructions for Operation Dig begin to unfold. He gives a warning. "Here's where deep reefs and coral extend sixty feet below sea level. Sail here in shallow water and sneak onto land. Stay away from the inhabitants.

"While you are there, you might see dolphin jumping about. Enjoy the siting, yes, but keep your focus on the plan."

"Captain," Calvin asks. "How many people live on the island?"

"According to my drone's detector, there are about twenty-six people who live on the island, including the seahorse. There are cottages for rent where you might find tourists, but the cottages remain empty most of the time. No one hardly goes there anymore. One of your most important tasks will be to keep the villagers away while you are digging up the body. Most of all, keep the seahorse away. Your goal will be to sneak in, get the dead body, and get out, before the villagers even know you are there."

"And if they find us on the island?"

"Come with me into my secret chamber. I have everything you'll need for protection." Captain Sam leads the three shipmates to a secret door in his study. "Welcome to the arms room."

Inside the private room, the walls are filled with weapons of all types. To some degree, the guns divert my mind from Stella's captivity. We congregate around a small circular high table, made of pinewood. In the center of the table, a pair of lenses set in a black frame lie next to a mechanical eyepiece.

"You wear glasses, Captain?" Walter asks.

"No. My vision is 20/20. This is a very special pair of glasses. It's made to hold an eyepiece." The captain picks up the mechanical device. He puts them on and takes them off. "The eyepiece has been designed to detect spy drones within 200 feet. It's lightweight, about 50 grams. When you fasten the eyepiece to the right lens, you'll be able to find any spy drone. I have three hidden in this room. Go ahead. See how fast you can find them."

Sam looks in my direction.

"Me?" I ask.

"You'll be the lookout while Walter and Calvin are digging up skull and bones. Try 'em out."

Walter picks up the circular framed glasses for quick observation, and then he sets them back down on the table. They look as regular as a pair of sunglasses from a drug store with a light tint. "Which way does the eyepiece go?"

"The hinge goes on the outside. Here's the power button." Captain Sam goes on to explain how they work. He shows us how easy the mechanical lens fastens onto the glasses.

I press the power button on, pick up the mechanical detector, and place it on top of the right lens. I feel a magnetic pull, and then it clicks and slides into position. It feels secure, and I put on the glasses. Scanning to the right, the mechanical lens faces one of the walls. I see a red light, identifying a micro spy drone on an upper shelf. I point. "Right there."

I find two more in less than one minute. "There's one. There's another one."

"Mention to no one about this. Here's the plan. You are three tourists, a young couple with a captain. I'll let you decide who will be the captain, but I dare prophesy it will be you, Walter. From one captain to another, I have pleasure in saying the seas will be kind. If I'm not mistaken, there couldn't be a better day to sneak in and grab a body on a lonely island where no one goes, and that's all there is of it. Mark my words, if you follow the operation, the rotten seahorse won't even know you're there. Follow the Rules of Engagement, only use force if necessary, and be done with it."

My phone buzzes. It's a text from Piper. "Vinny and I made it to the finals!"

19

JEWEL IN THE SEA

Cindy's World

On the starboard side of the ship, far away from the regular passengers, I am lowered into the ocean with a newly designated captain and my significant other. I hear two bells from the Dreamboat, knowing it is now seven o'clock, three hours after the teleportation arrival. Before the end of the hour, it will be twilight. As we sail away, I notice green lights down the length of the starboard. Our small boat glides onward, motoring toward the island where Owen had taken his last breath of life.

Never once do I question what we are doing. Operation Dig is an excellent plan proposed by Captain Sam, better than any plan I could have come up with. It begins with approaching the thirty-four square mile island on the southeastern coast at St. George's Bay. We are determined to blend in as tourists.

I navigate deeper into the open waters for the sake of the kitchen lady and the rest of the world. The miserable epoch of a detainee, whose name I am forbidden to speak, confirms my calling to sail beyond the nautical twilight hour, which is the first watch back on the Dreamboat.

The weather is fine when our boat sails away from the cruise ship. It is mid-August, nearly ninety degrees Fahrenheit, and I feel the sun beaming less on my arms than when I arrived in the afternoon. My hair is flapping in the wind. The immense ocean and vast horizon surround me on every side. It speaks of a power as mighty as the Almighty. At length through a telescope, I see land on the horizon. Over the next hour, I sense a need to shift my fear of the super ocean to loving the Ruler of the elements, here displayed in a most terrific guise.

I see shades of orange, red, and purple in the west, as the boat glides closer to shore. Beach cottages are lined up next to pristine white sand, forming a restful scene of beauty. Crystal clear turquoise water is rendered sublime near the rolling hills of this jewel in the sea. A once untouched tropical beauty on Earth, now offering a glorious resort, the coast looks inviting to guests, yet the surrounding coast shouts privacy from the inhabitations of an island race of beings. I hear brawling waves crash against coastal boulders, sounding like thunder cracking down on immovable rocks. The water splashes downward, plunging and repositioning in search of a new waterway passage.

Captain Walter drifts the boat slowly into position near the dock. Soon after, Calvin jumps out of the boat to loop a rope onto a hook, fastening the boat secure. This resort is more wonderful and worthy than anything else here on a charming island in the sea, the soft pallid sand makes it even more tranquil. I accept another illegal teleportation took place so far away from the mainland, in the middle of nowhere, tucked away where no one would find it except for Captain Sam's drone.

Walter looks at his cell phone, gathering data. "Rain should hold off until tomorrow afternoon. No detection of falling stars."

A tingling long-lost sense of adventure finds its way into my soul, washing over me before I set foot on dry ground. The wind whispers a soft melody of escapade in soothing accents. Nature bids me to not give in to a brash obstacle of distress. I suddenly take on my part as a tourist with an eager gaiety of womanhood. The lapping sounds of the water swaying against the boats act as a lullaby, padding my too keen sensations with comfort. Stepping out of the boat, I try out my new role in spite of feeling fatigued. "This should be the best weekend vacation ever. I've always wanted to climb a palm tree. Think we'll find any coconuts?"

Calvin acknowledges my new role with a quiet grin. "Maybe. I'm sure we'll find a whole lot more. Walter, you ever climb a palm tree before?"

Captain Walter plays along. "Nope. Tree climbing is on my bucket list. I rescued my neighbor's cat once, but we used a ladder."

"Are there any rules about tree climbing I need to know about?" I ask.

"Just one. Don't fall out." Calvin chuckles a kind tune.

"Time to check in."

Outside the wooden shop, we set our bags down in the sand. I think about Captain Sam's last words, *Be invisible*. For a short space of time, Calvin and I quietly wait near the stairs of the rental shop while Captain Walter approaches the doorknob. I hear him jiggle the knob and then knock. He looks into a glass window and waves when he sees someone.

A man opens the door. "We closed at 8."

"I know. I called a while ago. Are you Jerry?"

"Yes."

"I spoke to you on the phone. I'm Walter. I made a reservation and need to check in."

"Come on in."

Walter walks inside to fetch the keys.

Instead of forcing the role as a young couple, which does not at all feel natural, I stand side by side with Calvin at the railing, watching the tide roll in. Neither one of us knows what to say.

"I think this weekend vacation is going to be great," I say. "Want to know why?"

"Why?"

"I've always wanted to climb a palm tree." I say.

206

"I bet you were one of those girls who went on the monkey bars."

"I loved the monkey bars."

"You afraid of heights?" he asks.

"Not really. Wait. How high are you talking about?"

"Have you ever jumped out of an airplane?" he asks.

"No. Have you?"

"Five times."

"How cool is that?" I say.

"It gets your adrenaline going. Would you ever do it?"

"Probably not."

"What is on your bucket list?" he asks.

No one has ever asked me that. "Cracking open a coconut."

"It's not as easy as it sounds," he points out.

"Have you ever opened a coconut?"

"No. So what else is on your bucket list?"

I quickly think of something. "I'd like to bicycle across the United States."

"Impressive. So what else is on your bucket list?"

"I really don't have one," I admit.

"Why not?"

"I just read books."

"That's interesting," he says.

"And I like going to the movies. What do you like to do?"

"Yesterday, I would have told you that I like helping people."

"And today?" I ask.

"I still like helping people."

"Me too." I think Calvin is my brother's age.

Captain Walter opens the door and returns. "We're five blocks down, oceanfront, in the first row. Here's a key."

Next, I follow our captain. He leads us to a cottage where we will get a good night's sleep, a small two-bedroom beach bungalow. According to plan, we arrive at the door as quiet as a butterfly in a bucolic field of colorful snapdragons on a sunny afternoon. In the dark, I see a sign attached to the door under a dim light, a name for the cottage, Moonflower. Everything inside is clean. I alight and throw myself at this undercover task, knowing this mission must be carried out successfully. The day's events have brought exhaustion in my body and mind, which I have endured.

I text Piper. "Long day. I'll tell you about it when I get back. How'd the final race go?"

After a few minutes, Piper texts back. "Vinny won third place. I won first!"

"WOW! Way to go!"

"Thx. Night, sister."

"Night, brother."

A blanket of nightshade covers a solemn silence of this glorious island of imperial nature. My brother will finish shooting a Hitchcock movie, and I am going on a new adventure. I take a warm shower, place my head on a soft pillow, and sleep. When I wake up, we will hike out to do the unthinkable.

***

Back in the kitchen of the Seahorse Café, Catfish, Drake, and Burdock are sharing a delicious midnight snack.

"That's all I get?" Catfish asks. He pulls a piece of sweet tasting meat out of a pink shell.

"It's a snack, you dunderjack." Drake dips a white fleshy bite into melted butter. "Sam is missing out."

Burdock cracks open the last leg without any problem. "Want to cook another one?"

"No, mate." Drake "We don't have another one. Hurry up before someone finds us."

20

OPERATION DIG

Cindy's World — the next day

I wake up feeling refreshed. I lay still for a moment until I hear a voice in the next room. Someone knocks on my door. "Six o'clock." Someone knocks again on my door and I hear Captain Walter. "Cindy? You up? It's six o'clock. We leave in thirty minutes."

"I'm up."

I get dressed, brush my teeth, and crack open the front door to feel the temperature. The ground looks dry, and the air feels about eighty degrees. Either the natural surroundings or the secret task energizes me. I can't tell which it is. It must be a mixture of both. It's early. Soon I will be roaming on foot with Calvin and Captain Walter leading the way. I eat a nutty breakfast bar, drink chocolate milk, and then step out onto a porch. I see blue hydrangea planted up on a ledge, giving this bungalow entrance privacy. I hope Captain Sam's plan works because I need to get back home and finish my book.

We walk for a short while on the shore, enjoying the lovely sound of ocean water. At a slow steady pace, Walter follows the directions on his GPS, advancing us from the shore through rolling hills as the sun comes up. Finally, we reach a small valley. Twenty minutes after leaving the cottage, daylight has taken effect. I see a lightly wooded forest with squirrels leaping about in trees and birds singing in the morning sun.

Walter stops to take a drink of water.

"How close are we?" Calvin looks around.

"It's a hundred yards ahead." Captain Walter returns his bottle in his backpack.

I am watchful while I put Captain Sam's glasses on with two hands. Every sound catches my attention, and I resolve to find any drone from any direction. I scan while we make our way to the location of the buried cadaver. I follow along even though we have no knowledge to the location of our enemies.

Peace, peace. All will be safe.

Walter identifies the place where they will dig. He gives a speech to honor the life of dear Owen. He clears his throat.

"The sun and heavenly host above can bear witness to what we are about to do. Here lies the remains of an innocent victim. Digging it up is something we must do. We have to do it to save the human race from two crazy men. We are looking for justice. Owen died a wrongful death. He trusted the wrong people. He traveled into the unknown to become famous. If only he could have had a different goal in life. Nature has taken its course. Now he will be famous for a different reason. I know his human decomposition will be significant. We need all the tissue we can get. We are here. Sorry we are late. We are ready. We are taking these bones to a better place. Ok. Let's get this done."

"I'll start on this end. You start on that end." Calvin says in a serious, solemn tone. He and Walter shovel and toss dirt into a pile.

I stand guard and look around. Misery must have filled Owen's heart over what happened to him. There must be some way to find the person who is responsible for this crime.

After a while, Calvin stops digging. "I think I found Owen. Whatever happens, whatever he looks like, we will continue this operation all the way to the very end."

Walter reaches for his phone. "Captain? We found him. Send a helicopter, and arrest Cricket."

They put on a mask covering and continue to shovel gingerly around his body.

"Poor Owen," says Walter. "What did they do to him?"

"It smells so bad. Where are the legs?" Calvin asks.

"He doesn't have any," Walter observes. "Maybe they disintegrated."

I can't look at it any longer. The head doesn't even look like a human skull. If they can just hurry up and get Owen in the bag, the sooner we can get out of here. "Everything still looks clear."

Once Owen's remains are in the body bag, Walter zips up the bag. Calvin carefully picks up Owen, carries him under two arms, and we head back.

We hear a helicopter swoop in for a landing somewhere off in the distance. The captain has sent a Bloodhound in case Cricket attempts to escape.

"Wait," I say. "I see a drone."

"Where?" Walter asks immediately.

"There," I point.

"It's Cain," Walter says.

Walter reaches for his Rat and gets it out without any fear. "Get ready to run to the boat with Owen, and I'll catch up with you."

"What are you going to do?" I ask.

"I'm bringing it back. Captain's orders. Everyone, stand still. I just need it to get a little bit closer." Walter launches the Rat, and we wait until the drone flies within shooting distance.

Zing!

The drone falls to the ground.

"Nice shot!" Calvin says.

"The detector never misses. Goes right to it. Plan B: Run to the boat like your hair's on fire," Walter says.

Our pace suddenly picks up. Walter runs to retrieve the drone and captures it.

Calvin and I are the first to get in the boat. Walter soon catches up.

We sail at high speed all the way back to the ship.

Captain Sam welcomes us with a warm greeting. "Come aboard." He speaks directly to me. "Cindy, you're a natural sailor. Your friend has been cleared. Here is a gift certificate for helping Walter. I'd like to give you a souvenir. It would be an honor if you could keep the glasses."

I feel as if a weight has been lifted. "Thank you, Captain."

"Bend your ear to this." Captain Sam commands his crew. "Get that body to the morgue. Do an inspection. Cricket has been arrested for murder. Walter, see what you can do."

Captain Sam alone is in the position to give marching orders. When I thought of what had just taken place, my hope for justice increases. I neither speak nor look at anyone while they place Owen on a stretcher. I stand motionless, grateful for returning his body and allowing him to have a proper burial. Captain Sam's voice continued to give instructions, plain and simple. "And get a bite to eat when you can!"

Heavy misfortunes have fallen on Owen, but I must get back to Stella. I watch as they push the remains of Owen away, knowing what they will find inside that bag. A power so great had taken his life away. A greater power will now track down the criminals and stop them from committing any further illegal teleportation.

Two days later

Preparations had been made for our arrival at Nassau. As I touch the shore, I naturally let go of the past, but I hang onto my souvenirs. It was a scavenger hunt collecting all of them in my string pack, a Dolphin journal, pirate T-shirt, Eastern-tailed Blue Butterfly pin, Captain Sam's glasses, a brown bar of Muddy Salve Soap, a flying firetruck, Mudflat Garden map, USS brochure, the Four Spiritual Laws, and a Dreamboat lanyard. I see Danny one last time and say a quick goodbye. Stella and I find a ride to the airport and have no problem getting on board. Stella and I are having a nice flight home. We are each traveling light with a carry on.

Stella's memory is completely back with a greater determination to book more kitchen parties. She is talking to Vinny on the phone. "I couldn't eat anything until noon. Then they gave me coconut juice. An hour later, they gave me a smoothie with vitamins in it. An hour later, I had to exercise for one hour. They drilled me on several things for two hours. I had to sing the alphabet song, the national anthem, and amazing grace. Then I had to finish dinner by six. Then I couldn't eat anything until noon the next day. They made me exercise in the morning." She pauses. "Ok, see you soon."

I need to make a promise. "Stella, I promise I will go to another one of your parties this month if you promise me you'll go see another movie with me."

"Deal!"

Our plane taxis to the ramp. My double Dutch braids keep the hair off my face and let me rest my head on the headrest. My phone buzzes.

"Hello? Cal?"

"Cindy," Calvin says. "They finished the inspection."

"And?"

"They found a few things in Owen's DNA. They found time particles, black matter, and particles from a locust. I thought you might want to know. They think a locust landed on Walter's skin right when the teleport occurred. Walter has been questioning Cricket all afternoon. I'll call you when he's done."

"Thanks for the update," I say.

We walk down the ramp, pass by the luggage area, and move straight to curbside pickup. Stella runs to hug Vinny.

I feel my heart jump for joy when I see Piper waiting for me at the airport. Unable to conceal my feelings, I hug Piper with the most appreciation I've ever felt. My phone buzzes.

"Hello?"

It's Calvin again. "Cindy Sailor! Walter got a confession from Cricket. He's getting a lesser sentence for turning in Cain. Timberlake was never in on it."

"Great news! I'm so happy! I hope they arrest Cain. It's Cindy Smith. My last name is Smith." I say.

"Captain gave you a new name," he says.

The sweet burning sun is setting in the pleasant sky. We pass the city and head back home. I see my book still sitting exactly where I left it. My front yard looks the same, but the colors are more vivid. Sweet dahlias have bloomed beautifully in shades of red, pink, and violet. I walk up to my front porch where my parents are waiting.

"It's so good to be home! I missed you guys! I missed my bedroom, too!" I say.

"We missed you, too!" My dad hugs me first. "Come on in and tell us all about your trip."

"Oh, I'm so tired."

"We're so glad you're home! Come on in and get some rest." My mom hugs me second.

Piper walks inside after my mom and dad.

"I'll be in in just a minute," I say.

A soft air ruffles the summer leaves. It causes a pleasant motion in the tall Japanese Elm as I walk to the railing. My head whirls around to see my front yard. My steps were like that of a drunken sailor. It feels like freedom to be on dry ground. I wonder at our Maple Tree as if I am seeing my yard for the very first time. I see something I've never seen before. My neighbor Noah waves from across the street. I wave back.

I finally admit it. My life had been spared. In the end, my life really does not belong to me. We never step in the same river twice. This is a summer I will never forget. I can finish reading my book now. I begin a new journey, certain that whatever happens, things are going to work out just fine. I'll have strength from heaven to endure.

As I walk across the porch, I notice a beautiful blue dragonfly flutter by. I see it fly in an irregular pattern near the pink swamp milkweed.

"Hello, my little pet. Why are you flying like that?"

I put on Sam's glasses and scan my yard.

No sign of anything today. After a good night's sleep, I'll be ready to search again.

Four Spiritual Laws

ADAPTED FROM BILL BRIGHT, 1965

Law One (John 3:16, 10:10)
God loves you. He has good plans for you if you turn to Him and repent from sin. His plans are for you to have peace, joy, and reconciliation. He also has plans to give you special gifts unique for you.

Law Two (Romans 3:23, 6:23)
We all fall short of God's perfect standard of divine holiness. We need to confess this brokenness with a humble heart. We need to admit our need for God's grace and ask for a filling of the Holy Spirit each day.

Law Three (Rom 5:8, 1 Cor 15:3-6, Jn 14:6)
You matter to God so much that He sent his only Son as the Savior of the world to give you a better life. Jesus died on the cross to pay the penalty for all our sins. God wants a personal relationship with you because you matter to Him.

Law Four (Jn 1:12, 3:1-8, Eph 2:8-9)
Say a prayer to accept Jesus Christ as your personal Lord and Savior. Accept His new life for you each day with a humble and thankful attitude. He is the Light that shines the way for us. We are to shine our light for His name's sake.

Made in the USA
Middletown, DE
05 October 2021